BEFORE LIFE

A Collection of Short Stories

I0630213

TAAJI RAUF

This book is dedicated to:

God, My angels, and my Ancestors.
I hope I made you all proud.
Thank-you. Thanks for smiling down
on me and pushing me on my faith boat.

I love you.

TABLE OF CONTENTS

BEFORE LIFE

When I spoke to the Angels in my Before Life, I thought my request was well understood. I told the Angels to place me in Los Angeles California on January 1, 1989 at twelve midnight so that I could be the first child born in California of that year. I wanted to enter the world making history, and I also wanted to be the last born, the baby of my family. I figured that the baby gets all the benefits of their parents and siblings. I asked for a mother, a father, twin brothers, and a sister. I wanted a grandmother, but she died a little before I was born.

I talked to my grandmother all the time while I waited for the Angels to gently push me into the womb of my new mother. At the end of every one of my grandmother's sentences she called me, "little baby one", instead of saying, "You understand". I loved listening to my grandmother tell me about life with flesh, skin, and more eyes. Every time she sat next to me under my favorite tree, she wore extremely beautiful clothes; her clothes were colors that I would only remember after I left Before Life. At the end of every conversation, she always reminded me that I had to help my mother pass into adulthood.

I wanted my mother to be a singer and my father a poet. Singers are considered closer to heaven, because they sing the music of life. Music and melodies are the universal sounds of life, and every organism on Earth. Only a select few are truly blessed with the gift to sing life's music and melodies; I wanted my mother to have that gift.

I wanted my father to be a poet because he could define life through his words. I heard in Before Life that they have a dictionary invented by some guy named Webster, which people use to define words. I really don't believe in the dictionary, it is not as well respected as the poet's way of defining words. A poet has the ability to define the highs and lows of life. A poet can make an average person or scenario come to life through their words. I wanted my father to be able to expose me to the art of life; I didn't want to settle for the definition of life.

I yearned for my twin brothers to be philosophers, as they taught me through their intuition and spirituality. I wanted my sister to be a beautiful dancer who moved with a sensuous grace, like the river Niger in Mali. That was what I requested from the Angels. Everything else I would have to handle on my own as I lived to make each day better than the day before.

After my requests were submitted, I was ready to leave Before Life. I could not understand the souls who were reluctant to live on Earth. They usually had already lived many cycles on Earth. Some of their cycles had made them fearful of earthly life. I was thankful that my cycles on earth prepared me to want to return to the world of people with flesh and blood; new cycles meant that I had another opportunity to re-learn the complexities of life.

The reluctant souls used to scream and kick as they were cast into life. Sometimes they would purposely make themselves so sick that they couldn't live very long. If they concentrated hard enough some souls would stop breathing before they reached their sixth month of life. Some were successful in dying in child birth; I think doctors call children that die after child birth "still born". Other souls took drastic measures to ensure that they never lived another life. They would cause their mother extreme morning sickness, or push their way out before time, so that the mother could miscarry. While others sought out new mothers who carried DNA traits that predestined, leukemia or sickle cell and other dreaded diseases. Others wanted to speed to their death in their new life by finding mother's who had contracted AIDS.

The stronger souls were adamant about never living another cycle. These souls quietly whispered, "You should get rid of this baby," or "You can't afford to raise a child." That was the worst way of getting killed because they forced so many women to commit murder against their own children.

They did other things to die early such as tying the umbilical cord around their neck, or by refusing to breathe after they were delivered. I remember one soul who did not want to live; he stayed alive until he was five, until finally he purposely stepped in front of an oncoming 18 - wheel truck. He died happy because he was tired of life. He left his family with millions of dollars because they won the court case against the trucking company.

I was not reluctant to live, and I understood that life was not always easy. I was ready for the challenge; I intended to live until I was one hundred, as long as I lived well enough and treated my body right. I know that one hundred years is not a long time, but the things I would learn and see, would be phenomenal. I was ready to have skin, eyes, hands and feet.

As I waited in the gardens, I used to take the branches off the trees to etch lines in my hand. It was a myth among many of the souls that the more time you took etching the lines on your hand, the better your life would become. I deeply etched the line from the base of my thumb to the edge of my palm. I made sure that I didn't make any breaks or tassels so that I could ensure that I would have an enthusiastic life. I wanted my line to symbolize my courage, energy, and desire to win. I have seen some careless souls etch reckless breaks and tassels in their palm; they didn't even realize that they were making life difficult from their first day to their last.

I made the line that is in between my thumb and index finger straight with a sharp turn toward my wrist-- I wanted to be able to use my imagination. I knew that this line would help me be perceptive, better able to know how people think and feel. During my life, I wanted to always look to the future as I moved through the present. Finally I etched my heart line all the way under my index finger I needed to be a true romantic this life cycle, someone that is loving and lovable. In my last life cycle I was hard to love: I either shielded my love or I never showed it. I hated committing to ideas or people. This time I was going to be productive, nurturing, and devoted to my friends and loved ones.

Before I left to begin my cycle there were exactly ninety - nine people ahead of me. Everyone had to wait their turn. The line moved faster when someone died. The first couple of people left slowly. Then there was a surge because there was a war on earth. Some left screaming and others with poise. The line started to move so quickly that people weren't being born on their selected dates. Instead of January 1, 1989, I was born on January 2, 1989.

In the Before Life the Angels did not tell us that we had to wait nine months inside our mothers, before we truly entered the world. At first I was just an egg, and then a blob, then I started to develop. I was swimming in a circle of water were I ate, drank, and released my excrement. The water was always so clean, especially the more water my mother drank. When my ears and eyes finally developed, I started to hear and see people. I used to stare with my mother into her mirror; she looked so beautiful and young.

One day I woke up to singing men and women on her eighteenth birthday. I was surprised and disappointed because I wanted my mother to be a woman not a girl. Once I realized this I kicked at her stomach so hard I because I was so angry. She told everyone, "Guy's I just felt Bilal kick!" Well at least I learned my name out of the kick. My mom was going to name me Bilal, a man who was important to ancient world history in the Islamic holy city of Mecca. Bilal, was an African who had journeyed on the trade routes from Africa to the Middle East. After settling in the Middle East he became the first man to call Muslims to prayer at the Qa'ba, an expansive holy temple in the Middle East where people migrate every year. I learned world history from the Angels; there were many Angels that loved to teach everyone as we waited to start another life. My mom didn't even know it, but my name was a part of world history.

After my first kick, my mother would always let people touch her stomach so they could feel me kick. I hated that. When they put their hands on my stomach I would kick their hands away because they would block my view. My mom would just laugh and look down at me.

As my nine months of gestation time approached the end, I wanted to urgently be born. One day I started to move around frantically in the womb. I kicked hard and pushed against the sack's opening, trying to make the water burst. I made the water burst forcing my mother to let out a painful scream. She watched in horror as the water trickled down her leg. Her screams and gasps scared me, but she just did not understand how ready I was to leave her stomach. I kept pushing; my mom started crying, as she ran harder down the hall to the front door. She opened the door with a desperate thrust, making the cold air smack her hard in the face.

I saw a tall slender young man jump in a car and start the ignition of his car. I kind of remembered him from the party, and I knew he wasn't my father. I made a note to myself that I would figure out his relevance to my life later. He drove fast to the hospital while, my mother breathed hard. He took the freeway to make it to the hospital faster. There was so much traffic on the freeway that the Angels sent police to get us through the traffic. Two policeman on motorcycles got in front of our car, two cars flanked us on each side, and one motorcycle rode behind us. The police escort was perfect because I wanted to stop hurting my mother and enter my new cycle of life.

When we finally got to the hospital it reminded me of Before Life; everything was so white, bright, and clean. The people that were prepared to receive me into this world were so kind. I can remember the most special one, he wore a blue suit, his entire suit hung freely from his muscular body, the color he wore was similar to the color of the sky, and he smelled cleaner than fresh morning air in the middle of tall green trees. He spoke to my mother in such a soothing tone, "Relax, everything will go smooth, just relax." Her muscles finally relaxed, her breathing evened, she laid back and I pushed harder. I was ready to enter the world.

I didn't give the doctors' helpers' time to give my mother drugs. I wanted to come into the world as naturally as possible. I glided out as my mom's body voluntarily pushed me into the doctor with the blue suit's large, firm, and protective hands. Another lady that had stood next to the doctor the entire time extended her hands to wash me. The doctor walked past her, and cleaned me himself.

After I was clean and breathing properly, he handed me over to my mother. The doctor stared at me for a long time then he left the room followed by his helpers. When I looked at my mother she looked so surprised. I was too tired to try to understand her thoughts. I locked eyes with my mother then I fell asleep in her arms. When I woke up, I heard a woman asking my mother;

"Do you need clothes for your new little baby one?" She walked in with two large trash bags full of folded baby clothes.

"Yes, of course. Could you please leave them by my suitcase? Thank you so much."

"Not a problem sweetie. We always have enough for the little baby one."

My grandmother used to call me her 'little baby one'. The lady had on a yellow shirt and white pants; she looked like she could be one of my grandmother's friends, she shared my grandmother's passion for bright colors. After my grandmother's friend left the room, she left the sent of jasmine lingering in the room. Three men entered my mother's room: one was a priest, the other an Imam, and the third a Buddhist. My mom was so confused because she didn't call the men into the room.

"Good morning. May we pray for your baby?" The Imam positioned his kufi while, he smiled over at me.

"Do you do this for everyone?" My mother's shifted from the eyes of each of her three strange visitors. She had an uncanny feeling that she was very safe.

The priest clutched his Bible tighter, "No not for everyone. What is his name?"

"Bilal," My mother looked down at me and smiled, then back at her visitors with anticipation.

"That is a beautiful name; he is definitely a child of world history." The Buddhist man adjusted his robe, as he seemed to connect my name with the facts of history.

Then the Buddhist man began to chant in soothing tones, as the Imam lifted my small body toward the sky praying in Arabic. The priest blessed my forehead with a prayer, touching my forehead, and kissing a weathered wooden cross. After all the beautiful prayers were recited, I fell asleep as all three of the men smiled down at me.

When I woke up we were leaving the hospital early the next morning. The doctor in the blue suit walked us out the hospital; he even showed my mother the proper way to place me in my car seat. In the car my mother fell asleep and the man that drove us to the hospital was driving again, he was listening to soft rhythmic music that sounded like the beating of my heart.

I could hear him saying his own words over the beats of the music. His voice flowed uninterrupted by the melodic beat from the music in the car. His words and the music made a perfect union. I fell in love with the music of his words, with its heart - like rhythm. I didn't understand the relevance the driving man had in my life. I did not know if he was my father or if we had any blood relationship. I started to stare with my three day old eyes at the back of his slender neck as he drove to my new home.

He must have felt me staring because he turned around and said, "Was sup li'l man? I'm your uncle." I just kept staring at him in disbelief. He must've heard my confusion, as I stared harder at the back of his neck, because he turned around again, and said for the second time, "I'm your Uncle."

So that's who this man was, father or not, I liked him already. I could tell that he was a poet; he used his own cadence that was different from other prominent poets the Angels taught about in Before Life, such as William Shakespeare, Edgar Allen Poe, Paul Laurence Dunbar, Langston Hughes, or Amiri Baraka. It was becoming very clear that the Angels had not given me the family structure I requested, but the people had all the attributes that I had asked for.

When we went back to our house, she walked me to her room, and then laid me on her bed. I had been on her bed many times but this time I could feel the mattress and the soft fabric. The comforter felt like it had feathers in it.

I heard two knocks at the door; the door began rotating on familiar hinges. Two sets of foot steps entered the room. My mother introduced me to the twins; they looked like they were Indian. One was tall and one was short. The short one was eating a zirmosa, full of plump potatoes and ground beef. They started speaking in Hindu, but I could understand them. The taller one spoke first,

With intense concern he said, "That child is special."

The shorter twin said, "He will be strong."

The taller one replied, "He will need his strength."

They stared back at me, and then walked out the room. The short twin made me hungry. I opened my mouth to ask my mother for some food. No words came out. I then remembered that I was a baby and I couldn't talk yet. The next time I opened my mouth I started a hungry sounding cry. My mom rolled over and scooped me up. On instinct she unbuttoned her blouse and plopped her breast in my mouth. I began to suck and her milk it tasted so good. It was better than the things I loved while I was in her stomach. It tasted like honey, mixed with a little bit of nectar, and strawberries. It was so good. As I drank I heard her heart beat, and the sweet milk flowed from her nipple to my mouth. The rhythm that her heart was making and the steady flow of milk were soothingly guiding me into a deep sleep.

While I was sleeping I decided to go talk to the Angels since I couldn't talk to them while they hovered over my mother's bed.

I asked, "What went wrong? Who are these people?"

They said in unison, "Don't worry you will do fine."

One Angel continued to speak, "Listen carefully, your mother calls these people her roommates, your uncle is your uncle, but the others are your mothers roommates. These people are your true family. Do not despise them: love them. We did the best we could considering the circumstances."

"So I have to live with this family?"

"Yes, because you are one of the chosen ones. Do you remember the doctor? Do you remember the woman in the yellow shirt? Do you remember the three men?"

"Yes."

"We sent him to help you. They are an example of the help we will give you throughout your life. Some of the helpers will do more than others. Some will test you and some will teach you. Always remember to learn."

Although I could not change my life, I was prepared to live. I started to cry. My mother just laid me on my chest and my crying turned to an inaudible whimper. I heard a knock at the door, and only one set of footsteps. This time it was a young woman. Her skin was the color of tar and her eyes lit up the entire room. Her eyes seemed to dance when she smiled. I loved her immediately. My mom introduced her as her friend and my godmother. She provocatively twirled around our bed dancing to her own private music. She moved her thighs and her hips more than the rest of her body. She grinned and smiled as she danced. She climbed on the bed, taking an empty spot closest to my head, next to my mother's shoulder. My godmother made a joke and my mother giggled.

My chosen family labeled themselves as roommates, but we were all happy. This was my family my mother, my uncle, the Indian twins, my godmother, and me. As I thought about my family I started to feel overwhelmingly happy, my mom must've felt my happiness, because she started singing. I swear I heard my uncle putting words together making them rhyme, as my mother sang, and my god mother danced. Before Life was preparation for this life and this life would be another cycle so that I could re-learn existing. I was well - aware that during the after life I would be assessed. In this cycle, I was going to make sure that I learned as I lived.

A BROKEN VOW

From the time that I could remember, my life was one of those old choppy family home videos, filled with birthday parties, and pink trick candles. We use to film our trips to Ocean City, family reunions, and barbecues. It was at these places and events that I realized that my father didn't really love me. My mother and other family members always showed me so much love, but it was as if my father treated me as a consolation prize of his marriage. My father probably would have asked my mother to get her tubes tied before their honeymoon if he knew his first child was going to be a girl. My father didn't like girls. He really wanted to have a son as his first and only child. I used to always catch snippets of the grown up conversations or I'd watch my father's actions toward me.

One weekend we went to Ocean City. My mother watched me carefully in the water as my father aimed the camera at my mother's side profile. She yelled at him playfully, "Honey you have to film, Jocelyn."

"But, baby I want to film you." My father was in love with my mother's beauty. She was stunning. She was tall for a woman at five eight. She had long brown hair that reached the middle of her back. Sometimes she wore her hair in African twist or pressed. Her face was flawless especially when she smiled. My father was more than in love with her, he was enamored by her.

After my mother had admonished him, he half-heartedly pointed the camera my way, while he continued to stare at my mother. Another time I overheard my mother and grandmother talking at a family barbecue.

"That man of yours treats you like a trophy. If he wants a trophy wife he needs to make more money. Germantown is a nice part of Philadelphia; I just think the suburbs are better." My grandmother's voice was loud as she looked around the family room for any extended ears. I was listening very carefully as I watched television with my cousins.

"Mom, we manage quite well. Jocelyn has her own room and the family room is a great size for three people." By defending herself my mother was able to shift the conversation.

"When are you guys going to give me more grand children?" My grandmother continued to stare at my mother as she put a forkful of potato salad into her mouth.

"As soon as we save up enough money for a new house." I could hear in my mother's voice that she knew that another child was not going to fit into my father's family plan.

"A new house has nothing to do with another child. Samantha, I love you but, ya'll need a new baby in that house for balance. Harvey barely pays attention to Jocelyn. That little girl needs someone to play with bedside's you."

"Mama, Jocelyn is fine."

"Ummph." Her voice was full of disagreement.

I probably heard more of that conversation. My memory grasped onto the most hurtful part, "Harvey barely pays attention to Jocelyn.' My grandmother as usual was so right, my father never looked at me, and he only talked to me when we were in our house. When my mother spoke about my good grades, or my latest discovery at dinner, he always said, "Oh really", or "How interesting".

My mother always showed me her love. I didn't know it at the time, but my mom was preparing me to be a really wonderful woman. She used to always ask,

"Jocelyn, I believe that you are the prettiest little girl in the world. I am proud to have you as my daughter. I have an important question to ask you. What will you be when you grow up, Jocelyn?" Her eyes glittered with excitement as she anticipated my answer.

I'd scream with joy, "A teacher, a doctor, or the president."

My mom would flash her encouraging smile, "You can be anything you want in this world, just promise that you will always believe in yourself."

"I promise, mommy." I squeaked.

My mother had resigned herself to a career as a loyal housewife. Her life was filled with cooking, cleaning, washing, ironing, and attending my PTA meetings. Our house was always spotless; she enjoyed baking pies and cookies on the weekends. She did everything with great ease and her smile was constant.

One morning a drunken truck driver crashed into her car when she was on her way home from my PTA meeting. The truck driver rushed through a red light. The force and speed of the truck catapulted my mother into an oak tree on the side of the road. The force of his truck made my mother's car crack the tree in half. My mother was already dead when the ambulance arrived.

When I got home from school, a police car was parked in the drive way. My father was sitting on the couch with his head down. The police officer was holding his hat in his hand, shaking his head. I walked toward my father,

"Dad, where is Mom?" My dad didn't answer, so the police officer spoke to the back of my head,

"Your mother will not be coming home anymore."

His voice was so final, I started crying. My father never looked at me. His eyes were glued to an imaginary dot on the floor. The police officer picked me up and placed me on the couch across from my father. I don't know when the day became the night or when the police officer left. All I knew was that my mother was gone forever.

My mother was gone. My father was left to face his greatest fear, me, his only child.

At seven years old I buried my mother. During the funeral my grandmother told me to be strong, but I cried non-stop. By the time we got to my house for the wake, everyone looked blurry and out of focus. I cried so hard that my eyes swelled and became red puffy openings. My grandmother carried me to my room to rest. She sat next to my bed as I slept because she was afraid that I would catch a fever from all my crying.

I woke up in the morning waiting to hear my mother's footsteps approaching my door. All I heard was my father constantly changing the channels on our living room television.

That night at dinner my father ordered pizza. We ate in silence. I could hear the low hum of our television as cars pulled into their driveways. The pizza was horrible, it was cold, soggy, and it smelled funny. I could see the pizza sauce through the cheese. If my mom was alive she would have ordered a double cheese pizza, so that I couldn't see the red sauce through the cheese. This oversight by my father alarmed me, so I started my first and last conversation with my father.

"Dad? What are you putting in my lunch tomorrow?"

"Your, what?" he asked with such disgust, that I wish I hadn't asked about my lunch.

"My lunch for school." I continued.

"What are you asking me for, tell your mom."

"Dad, Mom is dead." Tears crept to my eye lids. The salt in my tears made my eye lids burn because I still hadn't recovered from the funeral. My body could no longer take my crying each tear felt like a needle piercing down my cheek. My dad pushed his chair back,

"Well, Ms. Missy, you will have to make your own lunch. I will leave a key for you on the table next to the door. Do not lose your key. Be sure that you leave school immediately after the bell rings."

He picked up his plate and left me alone at the dining room table. At seven I knew that my dad hated that I hadn't died in that car accident. I realized that my dad didn't care about my feelings. All he wanted was my mother to be alive so that he could continue loving her. I figured that my father was angry that I impeded on his marriage. After my mom died, I was a constant irksome reminder that my mom was gone forever.

My father stopped giving me attention after my mother died I only saw him when he came home from work or early in the morning. On the weekends he sent me to my grandmother's house. During the week days I dreaded every morning without my mother, I missed her waking me up with a slight nudge on my shoulder. I'd always wake up smiling as she opened my curtains. She opened the curtains even if the view was blocked by a pack of snow. In the spring and summer months she cracked the window so that fresh air could waft through my room. A couple of days before she died I remember asking her,

"Why do you open my curtains every day?"

My mother always talked to me as if I was an adult, "Honey, you have to look outside. The sooner you look outside, the sooner you can prepare for the day to come."

"What if I'm not ready for the day to come?" My voice cracked as it re-adjusted to being awake.

"You have to love the day, no matter the people, place, or circumstance. As you get older you will realize that love is your strongest attribute. The earlier you experience the day the stronger your love will become."

I jumped out of the bed to hug my mother's waist. I hugged her as tight as possible. My mother began stroking my head,

"Always, remember to love. Never lose love."

In that instance I knew that my mother loved my father unconditionally. I wondered why he hadn't learned to love from my mother. Her example made expressing and showing love so easy.

Now everything is horrible my grandmother comes over every Sunday night to pick out my clothes for the week because my father refused to help me get dressed for school. Every Sunday she had the same conversation with my father as he watched television.

"I miss her so much Mom. It's hard to talk to Jocelyn because she looks like her mother. I just do not want to feel sad every time I look at her. We both loved her so much." I had never heard my father speak with such honesty. My grand mother continued relentlessly.

"Son. That is no excuse for treating her like she doesn't exist. You have to start talking to her soon. She's got a sense of humor like her mother. When she's over my house she tells me and your father the best stories. You have to talk to her. It will help you learn your daughter. She needs you to treat her like your daughter, not like an abandoned child.

"Mom, I'll try."

My father never tried. At seven the person that loved me the most was dead and my father never tried to love me. In the mornings no one opened my curtains and I stopped dreaming of receiving love from my father, I only dreamed of one day leaving my father's house.

By the time I was nine it was the only dream that pushed me toward the next day. Every day I dreamed of having my own family to love, I vowed that I would love better than my father, and follow my mother's example. I had always hoped to start a family immediately after high school, yet I enrolled into college as a back-up plan. I needed to do anything to insure that after graduation I no longer lived in my father's house.

I finally escaped my father after I graduated from high school. I had been accepted into Howard University in Washington D.C. My first year at Howard was so exciting, with new people, places, and freedom. I even started to dream of becoming a successful doctor. Being away from my father's indifference, I was able to finally dream of my career goals instead of worrying about making him notice me. In college I didn't have to live with a man that never spoke to me or made me doubt my worth.

At Howard I was a great student and very involved in campus life. I majored in biology because I wanted to attend medical school immediately after college. I rarely went home for long vacations. If I did go home it was straight to my grandmother's house. I no longer considered my father's house, my home.

I met my husband Timothy during my junior year at Howard, during his final year of dentistry school. The old saying was true: "All young women find their husbands in college." "Maybe, not all I was just blessed". Timothy was so supportive of all my dreams. We even studied together. He would study dentistry, while I consumed all my biology textbooks.

During our study breaks in the Health Science Library or at his apartment I would tell him that I wanted to be a pediatrician. He'd get so excited, "Baby. I'm going to be a dentist and you'll be a pediatrician. We're going to be the modern day Huxtables. I'm going to have my own practice and you'll work at the best hospital in the city." I laughed with glee at the prospect that our lives would be so picture-perfect.

He gave me the love that I missed as a child. As an adult I had more control over the love that I gave and received. I was so happy that I had found a life- long mate. I knew that he would not only love me, but he would help me complete my secret vow, "To always love".

At his graduation dinner he proposed to me on one knee. He gave me a large sparkling diamond ring. His mother started crying and his father patted him on his back. I had no idea that he was interested in marriage so soon after college. During dessert I gazed at my ring and the new life that I was going to begin with my new husband. I couldn't help to look over at his mother's ring. My ring was bigger than hers. She must have felt me looking at her ring, "Don't be shrewd. The ring is only the beginning. Marriage is really the size of your love past the first appearances of grown kids and gray hair." All I could do was store her truth in my mind and smile.

Our wedding was gorgeous. We got married at the Georgetown Baptist Church on a Saturday evening the weekend before Thanksgiving. Our colors were black, white, and eggshell. The men wore black tuxedos and the women wore crème or eggshell dresses. My bridesmaids wore beautiful eggshell dresses and the groomsmen wore black tuxedos with eggshell cummerbunds' to compliment the ladies' dresses. Lines of white lights brightened the aisles and alter. Lilies and orchids were placed on the walls, aisle, and alter. One of Timothy's pretty nieces was the flower girl and his nephew was our handsome ring bearer.

I did not invite my father to my wedding. Instead I asked Timothy's father to walk me down the aisle. I convinced Timothy to wear a white tuxedo. We looked extremely elegant as the minister validated our union. After we said our vows, we walked toward the vestibule to jump over the ceremonial broom together. Everyone stood up cheering as we walked down the aisle toward the front doors of the church. Our guest threw rice and blew bubbles into the air as we got into our white limousine.

After college Timothy worked at a local dental office in Washington D.C. He supported me as I finished my last year of college. I had been accepted to Howard's medical school. As soon as I received my acceptance letter, I began preparing myself for the next fall. A month before graduation I realized I was pregnant. Timothy urged me to get an abortion because he knew that I really wanted to attend medical school.

On his leather couch one rainy Thursday evening we discussed my pregnancy.

"Honey. I support you in any decision you make. It's just that since I met you you've dreamed of going to medical school."

"I just can't abort our child."

"It's all about what will make you happy. I will be happy if you are happy. If you want to keep this child, then keep him."

"How do you know that it is a boy?"

"Did I say 'him'?"

We both got really silent and Timothy began to cry.

"Honey, I want you to be the happiest woman on the planet." His eyes were filled with so much sincerity that my eyes watered.

"I will be happy no matter my path. I will be happy as a wife, mother, and/or a pediatrician. Obviously, God has a plan for us and this child. We can't kill our baby."

"I apologize for my selfishness and thoughtlessness. If you really believe you will be happy, then I believe you." I knew that night that I would never become a pediatrician.

We now have three lovely children. Jonathan is the oldest, Nicole is our middle child, and Sophia is the baby. When they were babies it was so easy to love them because they needed my love. As babies they allowed me to feel needed and wanted. They all gave me so much attention and unconditional love. I was so proud of myself as I completed my vow to always love.

Once their personalities began to emerge, I began to stop loving my children. I only talked to my children when it was necessary. For me necessary occasions were family outings or in public. I made sure to play with them at family reunions and to give them hugs in front of their elementary schools.

When our house doors were closed, I knew I had no audience. I retreated to my bedroom to rest or talk on the telephone to my friends from college. I continually complained of being sick or exhausted. Timothy could not understand my fatigue he'd say, "You're at home all day. How are you so tired?"

I'd always retort, "Taking care of your kids is exhausting."

"These are 'our' kids, Jocelyn. All you have to do is raise them with love."

"I do love them. I just don't feel I have to talk to them to show my love." I expected Timothy to stop talking to them as well. His love only grew stronger the more I stopped loving my children. He gave me money to seek a psychiatrist. Instead I spent the money on clothes that I had to sneak in the house through our garage.

Regardless of my difficulties with my children each of them became very successful. Jonathan is a pediatrician; he has the career that I relinquished when I got pregnant with him. I hate him because he was able to live his dream. If I had aborted him I would have been a pediatrician instead of him. I used to purposely try to detour Jonathan from the science field. In fifth grade he made a hamster powered miniature city. I laughed when he showed me his finished project. He just smiled with hurt in his eyes, but the next day he came home with the first place prize.

He went to Howard to study pre- medicine. He graduated at the top of his class, joined the Alpha Phi Alpha fraternity, and married a wonderful woman. He now has his own practice in Atlanta and a beautiful family.

My second child Nicole is a phenomenal dancer. She is beautiful and totally unaffected by her beauty. She inherited her father's dark complexion and regal features. Her neck is long, her lips are plump, and her nose fits her face like a perfect button. Her eyes are big, clear, and always inquisitive. She does not crave the interested looks of anonymous men. With grace and dignity; she acknowledges the respectful stares and ignores the disrespectful gawking.

When she was four years old I realized my daughter was always going to be beautiful. I never told her that she was beautiful. Whenever I tell her, I make sure to use a condescending tone, "You're beautiful, but your butt doesn't fit your frame" or "Be careful of the colors you wear because you always want to be sure that your clothes flatter your skin tone". I used to tell her she was fat when she was in junior high school. I didn't want her head to get too big.

Her father always told her she was beautiful. I hated when he told her she was beautiful because I wanted to be the only beauty in his eyes. When she was about eleven years old I made a horrible assumption. She walked into the kitchen. Then my husband smiled and said,

"Good morning, beautiful."

I said, "Are you molesting my daughter?"

He slapped my face and glared into my eyes, "I would never touch my daughter inappropriately. How dare you disrespect this family with that question?"

After I was slapped, I turned to my daughter and said, "See what you did?"

She held her head down and ate her breakfast in silence. For weeks after that incident she purposely avoided me. After that morning she never looked at me like a girl. Instead she looked at me like a woman that understood the wrath of another woman's insecurity.

Nicole was the best dancer in our state. By the time she was sixteen she had traveled the world. I never saw her dance. I hated her too much to support her dream. No one had ever supported my dreams and I wasn't about to support Nicole. I wanted her to become a teacher so that she could hide her beauty behind snot nosed kids and parent - teacher conferences. Teachers are never considered beautiful always average. I wanted her career to strip her of her beauty. If she had become a teacher I would not hate her so much.

Sophia was the baby and she loved her mama. Sophia was also my strongest child. She was a born leader and she always had friends. I hated her the most because she didn't care what I thought. I used to tell her to stop jumping out of trees and she would just say, "It feels like I'm flying, Mama." She was a phenomenal athlete. She played every sport, but she blossomed in track. She ran above her age group in her track club. By the time she was twelve she was featured in her first newspaper article. She ran into the family room, "Look Mommy, I'm in the paper." I never took my eyes off the television. Then she said, "Don't worry I'll be on television soon."

Her prediction was correct. At eighteen she was in the Olympics. She won two gold medals, one silver, and a bronze. This time I had no choice, but to watch. Sophia became an international celebrity. She was always on the television, in magazines, and on MTV. When I got my favorite magazine in the mail, Sophia was on the cover.

I hate my children because they achieved and they never begged for my approval. They continued on their paths to success. The only thing that they accepted from me was my title as their mother. I hate that they don't need me.

My husband left me after Sophia turned eighteen. He moved to Atlanta to be closer to Jonathan, Nicole, and Sophia. He opened a prosperous dental office in Stone Mountain, Georgia. They bought me a house, a new car, and they always put money in my bank account. My family left me alone to wallow in my jealousy, envy, and hate.

Despite my beautiful wedding, our amazing family, and Timothy's love for me I still was satisfied. All I ever wanted was my mother to awaken me and open my curtains one more morning. I needed to hear my mother say one more time, "You have to love the day, no matter the people, place, or circumstance. As you get older you will realize that love is your strongest attribute. The earlier you experience the day the stronger your love will become." I wanted to jump out of the bed to hug my mother around her waist one more time, and feel her stroke the top of my head as she reminded me to, "Always, remember to love. Never lose the love."

THE COMMUTER

When my job offered me a promotion with more pay I quickly accepted the offer. The only downside was that I would have to relocate to Washington D.C. from New York City. I was hoping that I would have to relocate to a city that wasn't significantly affected by the September eleventh terrorist attacks. Two planes altered the lives of all Americans, especially those living in New York City and Washington D.C. After September eleventh the World Trade Center was named "Ground Zero", while The Pentagon lost one of its sides.

A week after the September eleventh, 2001 terrorism, I started to have a horrible nightmare. I named my nightmare "The Nightmare Train". I bought a dream catcher, special sleep oils from a Haitian herb shop in Brooklyn, a dream warrior statue, and sleeping pills. Nothing worked. No matter what technique I used before I went to sleep, I still had my nightmare. My dream had become my own private movie stuck on replay week after week. It was so recurrent that I created names for some of the people in my dream.

My dream started the same way every night. It was very simple in the beginning. Commuters got on and off the train at different stops on their way to their destinations. When each person got on the train they contorted their faces by putting their head down, chin close to chest, lips taut, and their nose slightly flared. I saw their eyes come alive with a different expressions and emotions.

I'm not usually psychic in my waking life, but in my dream I could hear the thoughts of Darlene a Black lady, wearing a yellow dress with red shoes. She sat in her seat staring at her life through the train windows. As the train sped along she thought in snippets about her kids and her husband. Then her thoughts jumped to her father with Alzheimer's in Ohio. Every night I wanted to cry in my dream as I listened to Darlene. She became sad because the last time she visited him he didn't remember her. She left his house crying and frustrated.

Darlene's thoughts went from happy to sad to happy by the time she got off the train. As she prepared to get off at her stop she'd think of her last visit to the bed and breakfast in Vermont with her husband. She'd reminisce about their hot baths together as they watched the snow fall outside her window. Then she would disappear from my dream.

I heard a girl I named Carly, thinking dismally as she grieved over her dead father. She had curly hair that she twisted and re- twisted. Her eyes became cloudy as she began to recollect about burying her father a week ago. Her father the light of her life by making sure he was active in her life. She was his baby girl. He pushed her to achieve and enjoy life. He took her to museums, parks, camping trips, and fishing. He was so happy to have a child because doctors said that her mother was not able to bear children. Her father wanted to have her so bad that her parents tried every night. She smiled at the love that her mother and her father shared. After two years of trying to have a child, her mother had finally gotten pregnant, unfortunately her mother died in childbirth.

Her father was a struggling single parent. They only went out to dinner two times a year, New Years Day, and Easter Sunday. That was the only time her father had extra money to spend on his small family. He took her fishing, camping, and bike riding. Every year he got her the same chocolate cake and an extra candle. On the first day of her period when she was thirteen, he told her to, "Remember that you are a lady, you are nobility, you have a heart and mind, use both. Do not let others compromise your life. You only live once."

I could also hear the thoughts of another man, Donald. His gray over-pressed suit, perfectly polished black shoes, and freshly cut hair proved his anal retentiveness. His thoughts were further evidence that he was anal. I heard him frantically ramble through his morning checklist. Listening to Donald was like listening to a schizophrenic's constant chatter with no breaks in between sentences. I could hear him repeat his morning "to-do" list. "Get up. Don't hit the snooze button, make the bed, shower, shave, brush teeth, and gargle with mouth wash." After he went through his list he remembered that he always forgot to use mouth wash. He'd yell to himself, "How could I forget to use mouth wash? Know everyone is going to smell my breath. Today is going to be a horrible day!" Then he would get off the train flustered, holding his lips tightly pressed together. After a couple of months of having my dream I used to think of ways to give mouth wash to Donald in my dream. No matter how hard I meditated on bringing Donald some mouth wash before I fell asleep all the events in his portion of my dream remained the same.

Every new passenger was unaware of the watching eyes of the old passengers as they searched to find a suitable seat. I could hear new passengers say the same thing for an instant as they boarded the train. "I am here, and you are here, we are here." New passengers held their heads down, chins close to chest; lips taut, and nose slightly flared.

I'd see mothers helping other mothers put their kids in seats and break down baby strollers. Young boys would give up their seat to old women, young men helped elderly commuters carry their groceries on the train. A middle aged man gave his seat to a pregnant woman, and then showed her son how to grip the hand pole next to his mother.

Then my dream truly becomes "The Nightmare Train", when a fat man with a blue T-shirt, gray sweat pants, and flip flops, gets on the train. His four hundred or so pounds occupied three seats. After he finishes positioning his legs, dozens of cans of corned beef hash begin falling out of his grocery bag -- one after the other. Everyone begins to frantically pick up each can. I had to pull my feet off the ground to avoid the cans.

Then my attention focuses on a little boy, Adam that I hadn't noticed in the beginning of my dream. He never stopped laughing and playing with his red balloon. His mother had dressed him in a white turtleneck and jumper. His eyes were as bright as his smile. His jaws looked as if they were full of the sweetest grapes and no matter the situation on the train he could always be heard laughing.

There was a teenage couple desperately in need of a hotel room as they kissed each other's tonsils out. I named them Susie and Ryan. Susie had on a long shredded jean skirt and a purple halter top. Her ears were pierced from top to bottom. Ryan had tattoos on every visible place on his body, he even had Susie's name tattooed across his neck. The black ink matched his black shirt, pants, and shoes. Susie's hand remained gripped to Ryan's inner thigh no matter how severe the jerks and jolts of the train.

At one of our stops a man in gray wool Brooks Brother Suit ran in vain for the train. As soon as he would reach the train doors they would slam shut on his face. He hit the train window with his brief case as the train sped to our next stop, leaving him upset on the platform.

In the seat in front of me were two college - aged young women wearing NYU sweat shirts. I named them Rachel and Aisha. They laughed uncontrollably at the man in the Brooks Brothers suit. Rachel always whispered to Aisha,

"He could have made the train if his suit wasn't so tight."

"I guess he thought that the Brooks Brothers suit meant that the train was going to wait for him." The two friends just looked at each other again and laughed. A very handsome, tall, dark brown skinned young man, wearing Timberland boots, a bomber jacket, and a New York Yankee hat. I named him Solomon; he leaned toward the girls, and said, "This is New York. He's going to have to work harder than that in this city."

He looked over at the two girls laughing, "You guys still shouldn't laugh at him."

Aisha flirtatiously retorted, "Why Not?"

"I wouldn't laugh at you if *you* missed the train."

"Is that right?"

Solomon always winked at me as he moved closer to sit next to Aisha.

A Cuban woman, Frederica began talking loudly on the train. Her brown hair was pulled into a tight chignon; she wore tapered jeans, and a t-shirt that read, "The Family that Prays together. Stay's together." Frederica clutched her Bible, while holding a bag full of religious pamphlets. She passed her pamphlets to every passenger on the train, her patchouli perfume lingering under my nose as I read the title of the pamphlet, "Will Jesus Return?"

After every sentence she said in English, she would repeat the same sentence in Spanish. In my dream I understood Frederica extremely well even though I only took Spanish for two years in college. At the beginning of her speech she would always introduce herself, "I am Frederica." Her deep Cuban accent became more apparent after every syllable. "My father wanted a boy but, ha I was born a girl. Mi papa' queria' un baron pero ha naci' hembra!"

I always tried to stare out the window to avoid getting caught by Frederica's eyes. She would stare at me until her eyes had successfully made me look at her as she spoke. During my waking hours, I used to wrack my brain trying to figure out ways to avoid Frederica's eyes in my dream. Her eyes were eerily hazel. When I looked into them I saw a reflection of myself. Her eyes were so unsettling, that I didn't want to have to challenge them every time I had my nightmare. Her eyes were dangerous since they were the threshold of her soul. They showed her thoughts, emotions, dreams, disappointments, and pain. She always waited for my attention before her next loud obnoxious comment, "Be wary of a person that doesn't dance. Cuidese de una persona que no baile."

If I were lucky I would snap awake when a girl I named Amanda started screaming. I'd get excited because I thought that my dream was finally over. On nights that I jolted myself awake, I'd go to my kitchen for a glass of water and was relieved that my dream was stopped.

When I'd fall back to sleep my dream would start from Amanda screaming. As soon as I looked over, I'd see Amanda screaming and hitting a man's pelvis area with her umbrella. "You fuckin' pervert." Apparently, Mr. John had shown his manhood in all its glory to Amanda. Amanda switched seats as Mr. John zipped his pants and ran to the back of our train car.

At that moment a transit cop appeared, I had never seen a New York City transit cop come to the rescue so quickly. Amanda began to point at Mr. John as she whispered John's indecency into the transit cops ear. The transit cop named Bob walked quickly toward Mr. John,

"Sir, you are under arrest for indecent exposure."

Then Aisha and her friend began to laugh uncontrollably at Bob's statement. Mr. John spit a mixture of saliva and mucus into Bob's face. He immediately radioed for backup. Then the two men began to wrestle.

Mr. John held on to a pole as Bob tried with all his might to yank his arm from the pole. As soon as the door opened at the next stop, Mr. John lost control, the pole broke from the floor of the train. Bob pushed Mr. John off the train and onto the platform floor. After our train doors closed, swarms of transit cops began to stomp, and kick Mr. John. Every one watched in silence as our train collected speed. The little boy Adam continued to laugh and play with his red balloon.

Solomon said to Aisha after Mr. John was arrested, "That looked like the fight scene from the Matrix II."

"Which fight scene?" Her eyes were intrigued by his observation.

"The one when Keanu Reeves was fighting in the playground against all the clones."

"I have never seen the Matrix II."

"Maybe, you and your friend can come to my house to watch it on DVD."

"Who's going to keep my friend company?"

"One of my boy's."

"I'd like that."

Despite the sweetness of the instantaneous love affair between Aisha and Solomon my dream got worse. A woman I named Binita, seemed very unassuming, but she wasn't unassuming at all. Her hair was pulled into a ponytail on the top of her head.

She was five feet tall and she had on a pair of white mule shoes to give her height. She was carrying a black purse and holding a grocery bag in each hand. She walked straight to a seat occupied by a Hispanic couple, Miguel and Edith. She walked up to the couple arrogantly, "One of ya'll got to get up!"

"No speakah, Ingles."

"You don't speak English. How could you not speak English?"

"We no speakah, Ingles."

"One of ya'll got to get out that fuckin' seat. I want to sit right here. You either get up or I'm going to sit on you."

"What?"

Binita then sat down on Edith and sat her bags on Miguel's lap. I had never noticed a man intently reading his newspaper. I named him William; he slammed down his paper, picked up Binita with one hand, and threw her onto the train floor. William walked back to his seat, adjusted his pants, picked up his newspaper, and continued reading.

Binita didn't say a word. She just lay in the middle of the aisle holding her purse to her chest and crying. I expected Binita to retaliate. She always stayed on her back in the middle of the aisle sobbing. Over Binita's sob's, we heard the conductor come over the loud speaker,

"I need everyone to be calm." I could hear him struggling with someone.

Another man came on the loud speaker, "Listen to your conductor and remain calm. We are taking over the cars of this train. Everyone must remain calm. I have two men in each car with loaded guns. No one will be allowed to get on or off this train." His voice was so absolute that I began to fear for my life. I didn't remember any suspicious men getting on the train at the beginning of my dream.

I frantically looked around the train for the two men with loaded guns. I noticed the two men that I hadn't seen before. They had on blue jackets, jeans, and white sweat socks. Adam stopped laughing and playing with his balloon when his mother pulled him onto her lap. Ryan and Susie stopped kissing, they were now gripping each other's arms, and they had unconsciously intertwined their hands together. Aisha moved closer to Solomon on their bench. Her friend Rachel moved closer to Aisha.

The man that controlled everyone's fate came back on the loud speaker and announced,

"Each car on this train has a bomb on it. We will detonate as soon as we are under, New York's famous train station." Everyone started to scream.

The man said in a menacing tone, "Screaming will do nothing to save any of you!"

Our train started to move faster toward the explosion point. The train shook violently as Frederica frantically prayed to God in English and Spanish. Other passengers were crying out, "Oh God" or "Please help us, Lord!" But there was no one to help us and our train was barreling toward death. We were going to be on news stations across America and the world. No one would know the real story. We would become martyrs, then praised as brave by family members. Everyone would hypothesize about our final hours, minutes, and seconds. They would all be wrong because only we knew the truth of our final hours, minutes, and seconds. At this point of my dream, I started to feel as if I was going to die.

After we were dead they would have no eyewitness accounts. No one would know the truth. Speculations and lies would be spread to assuage everyone's theories. Charities, Foundations, and memorials would be created to honor the people that died on this "Nightmare Train".

At the end of my dream the train exploded, I was hit by a pole. Adam's balloon popped and his little body torn into tiny pieces. The lovers never let go of each other, the remains of their hands were intertwined together on the subway tunnel floor next to Solomon's New York Yankee hat. Binita's head was decapitated. The cans of corn beef hash burst open and mixed with everyone's blood. The torn pages of Frederica's Bible were wafting in the air. No one or anything survived.

Every morning I would wake up surprised I was still alive, my bed soaked with sweat, and my pillow drenched in tears. My body would shake uncontrollably for five to ten minutes until I fully woke up. I would see salt tear tracks on my cheeks as I stared at myself in the mirror. I had to wake up an hour earlier every morning to get my mind ready for the new day. After a long shower that washed away the sweat of my nightmare and slowly dress for work.

After I paid my fare for the subway I'd wait on the platform thinking that I was going to step toward my death when I boarded the next arriving train. I never took a seat or looked into anyone's face after I got on the train. I always stood really close to the sliding doors and looked out the glass past the graffiti as I held onto a germy steel pole.   I watched the train pass illuminated exit signs and escape doors (which I counted every morning) as we zoomed toward my stop.

Every day as I walked up the stairs to reach the street nearest my office, I thanked God that I was still alive. To really thank God I gave an old homeless man with a wild beard, glassy gray eyes, who was draped in brown blankets three dollars every day.   With that gesture toward the old man, I hoped that God would bless my soul, and stop my nightmare from plaguing me every night. I wanted to have pleasant nights of sleep with beautiful dreams that I never remembered after my alarm sounded.

TOXIC URINE BOY

By the second week of school, Trevor, the boy I shared my desk with began to smell very toxic. It only took three days before I concluded that I was smelling urine from Trevor's clothes. His pants began to take on a yellowish hue that I knew was not sold in stores. Everyone in our class smelled Trevor. The boys named him "Toxic Urine Boy". He never cried when they called him "Toxic Urine Boy." He just smiled and played on the jungle gym with his imaginary friends. I hated having Trevor as my desk partner. The first couple of days that I smelled Trevor, I thought someone had poured ammonia all over my desk, my eyes began to water, and my nose began to itch. Thank God my teacher noticed my discomfort, "Are you okay?" Mrs. Becker inquired.

"No. Can I go to the bathroom?" In the bathroom I stared in the mirror hoping that Trevor's atrocious smell would go away, making the rest of my days as a fourth grader bearable. I returned to my desk. Trevor turned to greet me with a smile as I walked to our desk. For the next three days I made my eyes water, hoping that Mrs. Becker would change my seat. That tactic didn't work.

I was careful not to sit too close to Trevor; I didn't want his urine smell to penetrate into my clothes. Everyday I feared that at recess someone would smell Trevor on my clothes making me, "Toxic Urine girl" for the entire school year. If I was named "Toxic Urine Girl" and Trevor was already "Toxic Urine" boy,

I would have been scarred for life. I knew I couldn't handle that stress.

Trevor used to talk to me when our teacher wasn't looking. In order for him not to be heard by our teacher he had to lean into my section of the desk. With each word his odor got stronger. If Trevor needed a sharpened pencil, I gave him my sharpest pencil. If he needed paper I gave him a stack. The longer I made Trevor wait for his request, the more fearful I became that his smell would ooze into every thread of my clothes.

I never borrowed anything from Trevor, because his smell was steeped in everything that he owned. The pencils that I loaned him never made it back to my pencil box, thank God. I tried everything to get Trevor's seat changed. I told on him when he talked to me. I even forged a letter from my mother. I had so many misspelled words on the letter that Mrs. Becker knew my mother hadn't written it.

Even though I was only nine years old I realized that when Trevor announced that his favorite color was yellow, he had no idea that he reeked of the urine. A boy liking the color yellow was odd. He needed to stick to colors that weren't associated with urine, like maybe blue or green. Everything he owned was yellow. Yellow canvas shoes, yellow jeans, and yellow shirts with a green alligator on the shirt. The alligator looked like it was screaming. His backpack and lunchbox were yellow. The boy was obsessed with the color yellow so much that he smelled like yellow urine. I wished his mom would run him hot bath water every night instead of taking him to the store for more yellow clothes.

Mrs. Becker was a seasoned teacher at our school her rules were unbearable. She told us on the first day of school, "I will assign permanent seats. I will not change these seats for any reason. " She continued to ramble on about her reasons, but "assigned seats" sounded scary.   Mrs. Becker was dooming me to share a desk with someone who I didn't know. There were only five people from my third grade class with me in Mrs. Becker's class. Only Shauni, Jamal, Ali, and Samuel made it to Mrs. Becker's class. We were all excited to be in Mrs. Becker's class because she had animals in the classroom and she took her classes on field trips every two months. When my mother found out that I had been assigned to Mrs. Becker's class, room fourteen, she shouted, "Thank God."

That night I heard her talking to my Grandmother in the kitchen.

"Tanya is a lucky girl. The best fourth grade teacher at her school will be her teacher."

"That's good baby, now you can stop fretting about Tanya getting well educated. We have to use what we got. Tanya is using what she got, her brain. Let's just keep helping her so that she can always get the best."

I loved to listen to my mom and grandmother talk in the kitchen while I was supposed to be sleeping. They always answered the questions I was reluctant to ask either one of them. That night I understood that I was in Mrs. Becker's class for a very good reason. I had scored well on a test that I was given at the end of third grade. Well, Mrs. Becker was a great teacher and she always had the smartest kids in her classes, I was thankful to be one of her students, I just wasn't so happy about my desk partner, Trevor.

Everyday I day dreamed about a different desk partner, I wanted to sit next to Shauni. She was a quiet and uncomplicated girl. Talking to Shauni was like talking to a wall she never talked she only giggled lightly. Shauni was a shoe in for teacher's pet, she raised her hand on every question, she always volunteered to help, and she was always the line leader.

I realized that using the "talk too much" tactic was not going to work on Mrs. Becker. Talking to Trevor was going to get me in trouble, instead of getting him in trouble. I didn't want to loose my seat next to the window or get assigned penalties. I needed Trevor to move so that I could look out the window without smelling his pee.

Mrs. Becker warned us at the beginning of the year that, she would give us a lot of penalties if we broke her class room rules too many times. I remember the day she explained the class room rules,

"I will give penalties any one that breaks our classroom rules." Ali from my third grade class was the only brave person that shot his hand up,

"What is a penalty?"

All the rest of us were to afraid to ask, so after Ali asked Mrs. Becker we all collectively stared at Mrs. Becker waiting for her answer. Mrs. Becker pushed her glasses further up her nose,

"A penalty is a punishment that will make you think twice about bad behavior."

Everyone grunted but, Ali continued his questioning,

Mrs. Becker began to walk toward Ali as he started his second question,

"How many penalties will you give?"

"An appropriate amount could be five, ten, twenty, or twenty- five."

Ali stared up into Mrs. Becker's face and she stared down at him. He began to ask a third question. He stopped before he began by catching his breath and holding his lips together in order to save himself from Mrs. Becker's eyes. I really didn't need Mrs. Becker to answer Ali, but it was exciting to watch him challenge her.

Every time I thought of a new tactic to use to get my seat changed. I remembered Ali and Mrs. Becker's slight confrontation. That day Mrs. Becker won. I didn't want to challenge Mrs. Becker and I hated to lose. I didn't want to be at the other end of Mrs. Becker's eyes, so I always stopped myself from asking if I could get my seat changed. I was trapped forever as Trevor's desk partner.

I was frustrated by the beginning of the third month of school. None of my tactics ever worked. Trevor had become the bane of my existence. One day during recess I didn't feel like playing. Usually I'd be on the handball courts, but instead I positioned myself next to the water fountain. I was half hoping that I would get an epiphany and half hoping that someone would give me some good advice. Standing by the water fountain was the easiest place to start a conversation about anything from cartoons to understanding our parents.

For the first five minutes only fifth graders came to drink from the fountain. I made sure not to look at them because fifth graders were mean. They hated everyone that who wasn't a fifth grader. I guess they were mad that they couldn't be sixth graders. One day I saw a fifth grader push a little first grader to the ground. The fifth grader could have walked around the first grader. Fifth graders were just mean and bitter. I promised myself that I was never going to be bitter as a kid or ever. Being bitter was no fun for anyone and it wasn't going to hasten the elementary school clock. I knew that I had to take each year in elementary slow because being a kid was really fun.

Finally, the new kid in my class came to get a drink of water from the water fountain. The new kid was a girl. Everyone was used to the new kid being a boy, but she was a girl. She came to our class during the second month of class. Mrs. Becker introduced her as Phylicia. I felt so bad for Phylicia because she was assigned the seat next to Ali. Ali sat in the back of the class next to the door because he was the light switch and door monitor. Ali loved his job. He ran eagerly to the light switch when, Mrs. Becker told him, "Okay Ali, its time to turn off the lights."

When Phylicia leaned over to take drink of water, I noticed her red ribbon flapping against the wind. The two ponytail plaits on either side of her head were hitting her ear as the ribbon fluttered softly against her forehead. I had never noticed Phylicia's ribbons in her hair. I thought I was the only girl in my class who wore ribbons. I had a problem that needed a solution. Two minds were stronger than one, especially when they worked to reach a common goal. My goal was to get a new desk partner, any girl that wore ribbons in her hair like me had to be smart. It only made sense that the two girls that wore ribbons in their hair needed to sit next to each other. Phylicia and I needed to share seats so that we could have desk partner memories together.

I started to play with the green ribbons in my ponytail. Phylicia took forever to drink her water. She should've saved her juice box from breakfast to hold the large amount of water she was drinking. As soon as she stopped drinking her water she popped up and started staring back at me. We stood staring at each other. Our staring contest ended in a truce. She walked very close to my feet before she fell back onto the wall next to my left shoulder.

"How many different color ribbons do you have?'

"A lot." I responded with pure cockiness.

"Me too. My dad loves to buy me ribbons." She matched my cockiness.

"My mom buys my ribbons." I retorted proudly.

"Oh. My name is Tanya. What's your name?" She sounded very interested to know my name.

"Phylicia. Aren't you in my class?" I acted like I didn't know that she was in my class.

"Yeah. I sit next to the window." My voice started to deflate.

"You're lucky. I have to sit next to the wall." Her tone seemed hopeful.

"So, at least you get to sit next to Ali, he smells normal." The pain in my voice was evident.

"I couldn't imagine sitting next to Toxic Urine Boy." I could tell she felt my pain.

"You've smelled him too?" I don't know why I asked that because I knew that everyone had smelled Trevor.

Smirking she said, "Everyone has smelled Trevor."

"Why doesn't anyone say anything about his smell?" I wondered out loud.

Sighing she retorted, "At my old school the kids in my class would have made Trevor cry every day."

"Where is your old school?" I didn't know she was from another state.

"Philadelphia."

"Where is that?" I couldn't conceptualize her old city in my head.

"Far away, it took us two weeks to drive from Philadelphia to Los Angeles."

"That's a long time to sit in a car."

Phylicia and I were interrupted by the first bell. Our principal Mr. Kinney had created a two-bell system. On the first bell everyone had to freeze completely. If they were caught moving, playground monitors had the right to issue detention slips. As we waited for the second bell to ring Phylicia kept moving her fingers and blinking her eyes. When the second bell finally rang I said,

"I thought the principal said we couldn't move." I couldn't believe she was breaking the rules.

Her tone was matter of fact, "Of course we can move but, we can't do too much or we could get in trouble."

As we walked back to class I told her to meet me at the water fountain before we ate lunch. I knew Phylicia was destined to be a good friend. I was really hoping that she could give me ideas about getting my seat reassigned.

Phylicia met me at the water fountain like we had planned. We walked to the cafeteria talking about everything and I felt like we were friends forever. At lunch I complained about "Toxic Urine Boy". She just listened to me as I complained away stuffing my mouth with a bean burrito and ketchup. After we ate our lunch we talked about becoming desk partners. She hated sitting in the back and I hated sitting next to Trevor. So we decided to devise a way to sit next to each other.

The next day class was boring. After recess, Mrs. Becker did the less exciting subjects in the middle of the day. We finished up our reading lesson. Then we moved onto social studies which had more reading. I really love reading. Some kids read so slowly that it felt like I was stuck in a tar pit except I wasn't sinking.

I stared out the window until it was my turn to read out loud. From time to time I looked back at Phylicia staring past Mrs. Becker. It looked like my new friend was also bored. She didn't even respond when Ali tried to talk to her when Mrs. Becker wasn't looking.

We were handing in our social studies answers when the bell rang for lunch. Phylicia waited for me outside our classroom door. If it had been anyone else I would've gotten upset that they hadn't followed directions. Phylicia seemed too practical to care if she met me outside of class or at the water fountain. She knew that our meeting after lunch was important for building our plan. We ate lunch quickly and silently because it was the best lunch on the menu: chocolate milk, an apple, grape juice, and a pizza. I was silent because I was thinking about creating a "new desk plan" to get my seat changed.

As soon as we placed our trays on the belt we both raced to the water fountain.

"Phylicia I need to get a new seat. We need to start a "new desk" plan today. The urine smell is starting to affect my life. His fumes are stuck in my nose and I hate sharing my desk. He has all my pencils and I hate the color yellow now." My frustration was clear.

"I wish Mrs. Becker didn't have desk partners. At least we don't have to share a desk with a pencil stealer." Her tone firm.

"Ali is stealing your pencils?" I was surprised.

"Yup, it's horrible because we only have one box to put our pencils in and my pencils always disappear." She was clearly upset.

"You don't have your own pencil case." This was starting to sound like a problem we needed to handle at three o'clock.

"Yeah but, I use the pencil box so that I don't have to go in my cubby all the time."

Frowning I said, "Oh, I guess I'm not the only one that's suffering."

"But, Trevor is the worst problem of them all. Do you ever see him pee on himself?" She asked innocently.

Disgusted I responded, "No but, his clothes always look really damp."

"He is so gross." Her face was contorted as if she smelled him.

"I need to find a way to get him away from my desk."

Suggestively she asked, "Why don't you ask Mrs. Becker if you can take the empty desk in the back of the room?"

"No, I want to keep my seat next to the window." I really didn't want to lose my seat next to the window.

"Okay so we need to move Trevor out of his seat to the back of the room. I think the rest of our class will thank us." I could see ideas churning as her eyes sparkled.

"I don't care about the rest of the class. I care about my nose." I tugged at my nose.

"It does look like it is shriveling up." As I pointed and laughed.

I threw my hand onto my nose,

"Really?"

"I'm just kidding. Okay this seat change needs to happen today because I don't want to have another meeting about this tomorrow. I want to tell you about my crush tomorrow." Philylicia's eyes sparkled again, her voice sounded ready to move onto more important issues.

I began to tell her our plan, "As soon as we start our science lesson you need to make Shauni cry."

"How?"

"Throw a short pencil at the back of her head."

Phylicia bent from her waist as she laughed clutching her stomach,

"Why do I have to make Shauni cry?" She could barely get the questions out.

Proudly I said, "So that the other kids in the class will get anxious. This will confuse Mrs. Becker because she will have to deal with Shauni's crying while we are asking questions and trying to learn."

Confused she asked, "What will asking her questions have to do with getting your seat changed?"

"It will make it seem like Trevor and Shauni are distracting me. While she's trying to stop Shauni from crying I will tell on Trevor. I'll say, "Mrs. Becker Trevor is distracting me."

"That's it?" She had bought into my plan.

"Yup. Since Mrs. Becker will be so annoyed she will move Trevor because he is distracting me." My voice was extremely confident.

"That's why we have to ask all the questions and get Shauni to cry.

Convincingly she said, "I like this plan."

The first bell rang. Freeze! Then the second bell rang. We walked back to our class with a plan that was going to be implemented as soon as we sat in our seats. I squinted my eyes at Toxic Urine Boy. I was so happy that this was going to be my last day sitting next to him. For the last three months his smell slowly killed my sense of smell. I was reclaiming my sense of smell after the "new desk plan", was completed.

Mrs. Becker started a new lesson on clouds this was perfect for our plan. It would be so easy to ask questions. Ten minutes into the lesson, Mrs. Becker noticed that I was getting annoyed with Trevor. Every time he moved to ask a question I flinched, which scared him into keeping his hand down. Phylicia threw a short stubby pencil at Shauni's head while Mrs. Becker was looking at the projector. Shauni started crying louder and louder. I turned to Phylicia as she mouthed silently, "Ask her know." Her eyes were so focused that I blurted out, "Mrs. Becker, Trevor is distracting my concentration."

Other kids continued to ask questions, Phylicia was in the background jumping out of her seat to answer the questions, and Shauni couldn't stop crying.

Mrs. Becker sounded perturbed. She wanted to bring order to her classroom as quickly as possible,

"Who would like to change their seat?"

"I'll do it Mrs. Becker," Phylicia said while she packed up her desk.

"Tanya, today I'm going to move Phylicia to Trevor's seat. Trevor moved to the back with Ali. I want you all to be paired with people that are interested in today's lesson. I need to calm you all down. Hopefully the seat change will work." Mrs. Becker was very agitated by now.

Our plan had worked! For the next two hours we sat next to each other. I didn't smell, "Toxic Urine Boy" anymore. The next day Phylicia sat next to me as if we were assigned desk partners. It was just our luck that Trevor didn't come to school the next day.

Mrs. Becker didn't make Phylicia go back to her old seat. I stared out the window from time to time and we passed notes to each other. After that day we were as inseparable as twins.

When the recess bell rung we walked from our shared desk out of the classroom to the water fountain together. Phylicia and I leaned against the wall in silence for a couple of minutes. Instead of talking about "Toxic Urine Boy" I leaned toward Phylicia's ear,

Caringly I asked, "Who is your crush?"

Phylicia chuckled, "I'm going to have to tell you at lunch. Let's go play hand ball."

I clutched my waist and started laughing holding my stomach.

TO LOVE IN 1840

An old woman, named Thelly was talking assertively to a young girl. "Gal, you better run and get me two burlap sacks."

"Two?" The little girl's eyes almost popped out of her head.

"Look here, we got two women in here birthing babies. I need two burlap sacks. The way these gal's are breathing' I'm gon' need some help too. They might have their babies at the same time. Send for more help." Her voice filled with finality.

I knew this story by heart. My mother Betty re-told me the story of my birth every night until she was sold down the river when I was seven. She knew that I needed to know this story in order to always remember my birthday and my family.

She always started this part of our story by staring deep into my eyes. "You were born in eighteen twenty at the beginning of the summer months. I knew it was eighteen twenty because we had celebrated that year at the master's New Year's party. Up until I got pregnant with you I didn't pay attention to the years. I was so happy to be with child that I purposely remembered the year that you were to be born in. When I first felt you coming I was laying in the slave quarters on the floor. Next to another slave girl named Susan. She was already in labor. Susan was scared. I stroked her head and squeezed her hand to help her relax." She would always pause here as she thought back to that night.

Thelly helped both of us get ready to have our children. I felt comfortable with her because she helped every woman on the plantation have their children. She even helped our slave master's wife have her children. I remember her repeating in soothing tones, "Breathe slow and easy, new life is coming." As our pains came harder and quicker she looked at both of us sprawled out on the floor. "It look's like these two chillun are tryin' to come at the same time."

She was right. After a while I got up to go outside. I found a clear patch of grass under an oak tree. The moon and stars were shining hard onto my stomach. This little dark girl followed me outside with a burlap sack in her hand, "That sho is gon be a special baby." I smiled and started to breathe slowly. I heard the other girl scream a muted scream as I put my head back and then I pushed hard. You came out of me slow and easy. I could hear the other girl's baby crying from the cabin. You never cried. You just lay in my arms. We just looked into each others eyes. I placed you in the hard burlap sack that holds chicken feed before it was re- used as a slave child's baby blanket. You didn't even move as the sack scratched your soft body.

The little girl ran into the cabin and then she ran back to our tree. "Susan had a boy. She named him Thomas." I chuckled. The three of us just sat under the tree. We watched the leaves of the oak tree float in the wind. We looked at the moon and the stars in silence. I could tell you were searching for the North Star, so I pointed it out to you and said, "That star represents freedom. Follow the North Star to freedom, your freedom will come from your heart, my Star. Your heart is as free as the North Star." I named you Star right there under the stars. I didn't want you to get the master's name first. The master named you Sue later that day."

My mother always paused at this point in the story, "You need to always answer to Sue. I lifted you to the stars and prayed that you would live to have a husband, a family, and many children. Then she would end our story with her favorite saying. "Your heart is as free as the North Star."

Our master sold my mother when I reached my seventh year on the plantation. I was taking water from the well to the people in the fields when the overseer yelled, "Com' on Betty."

"We are takin' you to the Big House." Other slaves were standing over by the beginning of the trail to the, 'Big House'.

"Where we go'in massa?"

He raised his voice, "Ya'll getting sold today. Ya'll gon make me some money."

I started to shake. My mother looked intently at me, willing me not to cry, or make a scene. I didn't. I stood in horror as my mother was being taken from me.

We couldn't speak to each other, which made our separation unbearable. I felt like my heart was being torn out by a wild bear.

I ran to the oak tree where I was born. We sat under the tree on cool nights as she told me the story of my birth. I sat on my knees with my back side touching the heel of my feet. I leaned close to the green grass to cry my mother back. Even though I knew no tears would ever make her return to me. I stayed under the tree all day and night. I slept on my back facing the stars. That night I dreamt that I was as free as a star.

~ * * * ~

Years later when I myself was sold my Auction Paper's Read:

Brown female slave.

Able to bear children.

Straight teeth.

Called Sue.

Can be used in the house or the fields.

I was the last slave bought at the auction. There was a young male slave who wore shredded pants and no shirt. He was strong and healthy. Every time he moved a new muscle appeared. A ten year old boy with one ear was bought at the auction as well. I later found out that his old master had cut his ear off because he was caught listening to some white children learning how to read. A middle aged woman and a pregnant girl were bought together. Both of the women knew how to sew the finest clothes in North Carolina. We all had to share the small wagon with two hunting dog. If we ran for our freedom they would become our worst enemies.

We were all bunched in the back of the wagon. My knees were smashed against my breast; my torso was pressed between the hunting dogs, and oil tins. The southern sun was yellow hot. The landscape had green rolling hills and animals that were freer than a new born slave. I watched cardinals fly off of pine oak and evergreen tree branches into the sky.

After many hours we approached the road winding towards the big house on the new plantation. The road was uneven and rocky. I tasted salt on my lips as dust swirled around our wagon. Each time I inhaled my lungs were flooded with the salty air. The men driving the wagon started talking,

"Eighteen forty- four will be a great year for us." The older man proclaimed as he tilted his head back to take a drink from his metal flask.

"Boy, it's almost the middle of the year and we still doing the same job, transporting slaves from Raleigh to Pitt County." The older transporter didn't seem as content as I expected.

I listened intently to my transporters. They told me the year I was in and that my new plantation was in Pitt County. From the time I was seven, I started picking twigs at the beginning of the summer. I'd find the perfect twig to add to my bundle. I'd picked my newest twig on the last plantation. I knew that I was twenty- four and my transporters had even helped me confirm my age.

A young light brown skinned man in short trousers that probably belonged to the master and a large white shirt was brushing the mane of a magnificent horse. The saddle was shining from the glare of the sun. A middle aged white man with gray hair and a freshly trimmed beard swung the screen door open as he called out,

"Ya'll here mighty late.   I was expecting ya'll yesterday morning." His haughty tone was extremely vain.

"You know we had to travel the one hundred sixty or so miles from Raleigh."   The older transporter talked with my new master.   He talked quickly to ensure that he wasn't further scolded for being late.

"We haven't had rain in a long time, so I'm sure the roads were easy to travel across.   I'm going to have to cut a small portion of your pay off." His voice was final.

"There's no need for a pay cut.   We brought all of your slaves to you in one piece. We didn't even mess with your gal slaves." His reply was not heard by my new master. I prayed that he was not as unrelenting as he sounded.

"I'm going for a ride through my plantation.   Take these shackles off my new slaves and take them to the slave quarters."   Without any more words we were driven quickly to the fields.

We were let off at the edge of the tobacco fields. All I could hear was the rustle of hands tugging at tobacco leaves. We walked over to the water well where we were given a cup of water by a five year old little girl with a burlap sack as a dress. An old blind slave handed each of us a sack to collect the tobacco. We were expected to fill up our sacks by sundown. My entire body ached from my ride on the wagon, yet I started picking the tobacco slowly. With each reach and tug my entire back contracted and retracted in pain. I picked tobacco in silence following the lead of the other slaves.

As I picked tobacco on my new plantation, I decided that I was ready for love. I was tired of hating myself, the overseer, the master, the mistress, and every other slave. I didn't want the master's control my feelings any longer. I was going to find and experience love on this new and odd plantation.

My first master took my mother and my heart away when I was seven. I was going to take my heart back and love. I declared to myself that I was not going to worry about the pain of being a slave. Instead I was going to give and receive love. I remembered my mother telling me when I was younger, "Your heart is as free as the north star."

I looked forward to sundown because I had people to meet. I had to meet the young man that carried an elderly man from the fields to the quarters. I wanted to hear the pregnant slave that complained about her aching back. I wanted to meet the women that were in charge of the caldron pots. This was my new home. Letting love in would require me to love my new home.

The first person I met was the woman at the caldron pots. Her name was Betty the same as my mother. She smiled with her two front teeth missing as she filled my bowl with grits. I smiled back at her. I walked toward the back of the quarters searching for a patch of green grass to rest and eat. I sat watching black clouds tumble into lighter clouds. The green leaves on the tops of the trees waved slowly at first, then quickly in the sky. It looked like the leaves were trying to float with the wind, but the branches were holding on tightly to them. Pellets of rain began to drop into my bowl of grits.

The clouds burst suddenly. I didn't realize that I was getting soaked in the rain until the same young man that had carried the elderly man to the cabin was standing with me under the tree. He spoke to me through his smile,

"Don't you see that it's raining?" His smile only ended after his question was complete.

The people on this plantation loved to smile so I smiled back,

"It happened so fast that, I didn't notice."

His large frame and height shielded me from the rain as he stepped closer to my feet. His skin was perfect. It looked like his skin was pulled carefully over each bone on his face. His complexion was so even and creamy. When he smiled the skin on his cheek bones shined under the moon light. His eyes were very dark brown almost black. They were so welcoming that I immediately felt comfortable. His lips looked like two Indian canoes. They curved over his teeth when he talked and smiled.

"Let's move to that oak tree. It might keep us from most of this rain." I was so happy to find an oak tree because oak tree's reminded me of my mother.

I walked to the trunk of the tree, with the handsome young man walking next to me. He spoke first after we sat under the leaves of the tree,

"So are you new?" I could tell that he knew I was new by the way he examined my body especially my eyes.

"Yes, I just got here today." I hoped that he heard the dread in my voice as I answered his question. Being a slave was hard especially being sold from plantation to plantation

"Do you know where you are?"

"I know that we are in Pitt County, next to a river or even the ocean." I smiled at him with as many teeth as I could find in my mouth.

"Well you are smart, we are in Pitt County, and the Atlantic Ocean is at the front of the Big House." He was proud that he could give me so much information. I noticed him stick his chest out like the roosters do early in the morning.

"We are next to an ocean?" I had never seen the ocean. I wasn't quite sure if I was ever going to see the ocean. I didn't know my new slave master at all. I wasn't sure if he was mean, cruel, or both. Keeping his slaves from seeing the ocean would have been another restriction.

"Yup. That's why the air around hear smells like salt." That explained the salt that was in my lungs and on my lips when I first arrived on the plantation.

"I was sold here a couple of days ago and I had to ask a lot of questions to know what you already know. What's your name?"

"They call me Sue." I said in a whisper, "but my name is Star."

"They call me Tom," he replied in a whisper, "but my name is Thomas. My mama wanted me to have a dignified name." Thomas stared at me for a long time, before he asked,

"Where are you sleeping?"

"I don't know. They sent me to the fields as soon as I got here."

"You can sleep in my quarters, it's kind of crowded. Ever since I got here, I started to take care of some of the orphaned children. I tell them stories to help them sleep. In turn they keep a space in the corner for me to sleep. I'll make space for you, Star. Come on."

We started to walk together. Thomas led me to his quarters.

I knew I didn't have to ask any questions, but I wanted to break the silence, "Where are your quarters?"

"Its two slave quarters' down, then three slave quarters away from the fields." He stopped before his next sentence, "I have to walk alone because no one can see us walk together."

"No one is watching us right know. We are the only people still standing in the rain." I laughed lightly through my smile.

He looked around, listening for any awkward movements, "Well let's walk quickly."

We entered the crowded cabin. The floor was covered with crushed autumn leaves and burlap sacks. We walked over to a free corner behind some of the children in the cabin. None of the other adult slaves wanted to sleep near the orphaned children because many feared that the children would get attached. Thomas did not harbor this fear and he cheerfully made his bed in the same corner with the orphaned children. As he made my pallet to sleep on he started talking again, "I try to watch over these kids as best as I can." When we laid down a little boy moved over to give us more room.

I felt so comfortable with Thomas. We were careful to not speak while we were outside of the cabin. We talked late into the night every night. We did not want any of the slaves, the overseer, or the master to get suspicious of our friendship. Thomas did find a way to work across from me on the next tobacco patch. Thomas watched me from his patch as I glanced back at him out of the corner of my eye. I was falling in love with Thomas and he was falling for me. Love was all that we had and we found each other in time to love one another.

One night I whispered my "birthing" story to him. Thomas was very intrigued by my story, especially the part about the other baby.

"What plantation were you born on?

"In eastern North Carolina."

"I've been sold to plantations in every corner of North Carolina. I believe that I was born on a plantation in eastern North Carolina too. My mother was sold while I was very young and I never knew her."

I reached up to stroke his cheek as he continued talking, "One of the old ladies used to tease me because she said I was special."

"Do you know why she said you were special?"

"She used to tease and tell me that I was born with my soul mate. I didn't know what she meant, but your story sounds so much like mine. Star, I think I was the other baby born with you. What was the name of the other baby born that night?"

"Tom....Thomas. Thomas it was you. The other baby's name was Thomas. The old lady's name was 'Thelly'. She helped both our mothers. Thomas we found each other again." I was so happy that I wanted to scream and rejoice loudly. Instead I kissed Thomas sensually on his soft lips.

"Let me show you something," Thomas pulled out a roll of twigs and then I pulled out my roll of twigs.

"You keep a roll of twigs just like me!" I exclaimed. We began to place each twig side by side. After we laid out all the twigs we had the same amount of twigs. I continued to stroke Thomas' face, as I looked into his eyes as far as my eyes could reach.   He fell asleep with his face in my hands and we woke up that way. After we realized that we were born on the same night and on the same plantation. We were only separated by our bodies. Our hearts and minds were already united.

During the day we kept our distance as we snuck loving glances at each other.   When I complained that my hands were sore from picking tobacco. Thomas rubbed my hands. If his back ached, from crouching his large body over the tobacco leaves, I'd rub his back until he fell asleep.   We learned each other every night either by touching or telling each other stories. One night we had to find privacy away from the children. That night we learned much, much, more about each other.

On that clear night Thomas and I walked to the same oak tree that had shielded us from the rain on the first night we met. As we sat on the glistening green grass, Thomas leaned on his arm, "Star will you be my wife?"

I started to cry but nonetheless was able to say with a smile, "Yes."

We laid back into the grass, which cradled our bodies as Thomas undressed my body. His strong brown hands glided across my skin, from my feet to the space between my eyebrows. After his hands had caressed my body he kissed me from the space between my eyebrows to the top of my toes. I was moaning lightly and smiling. Thomas' eyes stayed fixed on exploring every part of my body. I wanted to have all of his children. Being with Thomas was going to be my heaven on earth.

We made slow, passionate love. I matched his every move, and soon our hearts were beating at the same rhythm. I loved and adored him with my entire body. I used my hands, my tongue, and my hair to feel Thomas. He moved me under, on top, and on the side of him. Our love making ended when the first red- orange strand of dawn was visible in the morning sky. The ring of the morning plantation bell startled us out of our sleep, reminding us of our days work.

That evening Thomas walked me under the oak tree again and we made silent love again. Again, we made love as if we were going to be separated from each other for an eternity. We were never separated, thank God, and our love only grew stronger and my belly began to expand.

An older woman on the plantation told me one day by the drinking well, "You are going to have twins." As my stomach grew and became heavier to carry, her intuition was correct. Thomas and I made love in different ways, but always with the same purpose, to be next to each other.

As fall turned to winter we found ways to love each other inside the cabin. We whispered into each other's ears, rubbed the aches away from one another. He rubbed my stomach to feel the babies kick or we had competitions to see who could tell the best stories to the orphans.

One night Thomas gave me a braded leaf bracelet, "This is a symbol of us. You are my wife. I love you with all my heart." I cried into his chest as he placed the bracelet around my twenty-four twigs. He placed the bracelet and the twigs back into my dress, as we hugged each other to sleep.

Two months later, I gave birth to twins--a boy and a girl. We wanted our children to experience freedom one day so we named our son, 'North' and our daughter, 'Star'. I told Thomas in a whisper late one night when the entire plantation was asleep, "I can't wait to say, 'Come to mama North, Star.' He laughed lovingly as he played with North and Star's tiny toes.

BLACK ROBIN HOOD

Ellis began his street hustlin' in Washington D.C. at the age of eleven, when he realized that he didn't want to live and die in Ledroit Park on 2ⁿᵈ and Elm Street Northwest.

His grandmother's house was between two college dorms. He observed the college kids' arrogance as they walked down his street. Both their faces and body language showed their distaste as they stepped over trash with their noses arched to the sky. Ellis grew up in a row house that was attached to an abandoned gray two- story house where crack heads and rats dwelled undisturbed. When he closed his eyes to go to sleep, either he would hear the shrieks of rats killing other rats for food, or exhalations as the crack heads found relief in their beloved pipes. Regardless of the weather, his street always looked gray. In the winter he could see the cold gray air as he breathed. In the summer he could see the steamy gray heat rise from the concrete.

He knew that the college up the block was a goal he could attain after high school, but Ellis also realized that he needed money to help his grandmother take care of his little brothers, the twins Marcus and Daniel. The "Say No to Drugs" programs at his elementary school taught him that drugs were bad, but Ellis needed to make money for his family.

His first hustle was at the bottom of the ranks as a "Street Watcher" for any suspicious vehicles, people, and police street cruisers. Ellis sat on his bike with his arms over the handle bars at the corner of Second and Elm as his eyes protected the older drug dealers from the cops and rival drug gangs.

Ellis circled the block on the BMX ten-speed that he got for Christmas from his grandmother. Older drug dealers requested his services during important deals because he watched everything. He watched the black cats that crossed the street and the postman delivering mail after five. He was highly gifted in this line of work. He could hear sirens approaching from the fire station on Florida Avenue, he could read lips, discern the true character of any one, and his peripheral vision was exceptionally clear.

Despite becoming deeply entrenched in the ruthlessness of the drug world, Ellis maintained his compassion. One cold morning he stepped outside after a hard snow storm, bundled up in his winter coat, gloves, scarf, and hat that the drug dealer he was working for bought for him. On his way to middle school he saw another boy walking to school, shivering in only a long-sleeved shirt. Ellis stopped the shivering boy to give him his gloves and scarf. The boy's name was Earl. He was already in his first year of high school, Ellis later learned that Earl's mother was a crack head, and she never bought anything for her son or his three younger sisters. After that day, Earl and Ellis were inseparable. If Earl heard of anyone looking at Ellis the wrong way, that person would be greeted with a huge, black fist when the three o'clock bell rang. Ellis used to sneak food from his grandmother's house to give to Earl. Ellis' constant gestures of kindness made Earl eternally grateful for his new friend.

Ellis was good at finding street surveillance's, or cops undercover as addicts. One Saturday morning while eating cereal with Marcus and Daniel, he looked into the rooming house across the street and saw a camera peeking from behind the drapes. Since, he knew every person in every house on the street. He surmised that the camera was coming from the room on the third floor. He finished his cereal, grabbed his bike and rode up and down the street announcing, as if singing a song in a normal tone of voice, "Po-Po's in the rooming house".

Slowly everyone retreated from the corner and Ellis purchased some more milk for his grandmother from the yellow painted corner store. The police never figured out who tipped off the drug dealers, but the police chief had to explain the death of five undercover cops.

Ellis possessed many special gifts. Had he been born in the suburbs, he might have been deemed a prodigy. Being a watcher for the drug dealers only happened after school and on weekends. His grandmother held education in high regard and she expected her grandchildren to attend school every day. Neither he nor his brothers missed a day. Ellis took advantage of his school days. Every day Ellis dropped his little brothers off at their elementary school by seven a.m. so that they could eat the free breakfast. Then, he walked the two blocks to his middle school to eat his free breakfast.

They ate breakfast at school so his grandmother could have more money for dinner and weekend meals.   He didn't mind getting up early because breakfast was his favorite meal. After he ate the standard-issue breakfast of boxed cereal and milk, he was the first and only kid who ventured inside the school library.

During these quiet times in the library he read the autobiographies of as many great men as possible, from Benjamin Banneker to Malcolm X. The librarian, Mrs. Flowers, noticed that he always finished each book by the end of the week. She had to force him out of the library when the eight a.m. bell rang,

"Ellis the bell has sounded. Go to class."

"Mrs. Flowers please let me finish this chapter." As much as she wanted to let Ellis stay in the library, she had to abide by the school rules. Ellis never told Earl that he loved to read, but Earl knew that he had a very different kind of friend.   Earl knew that Ellis had a very smart and intelligent mind.

Mrs. Flowers knew that Ellis was special. Up until his eighth grade graduation she did everything she could to help nourish his mind. If Ellis was reading about The Great Depression, she bought him books about the migration of African Americans from the South to the North. When he started reading about slavery she gave him a copy of the Declaration of Independence and the Constitution. The same day she gave him the constitution he memorized the first ten amendments by lunch time. He walked into the library during lunch,

"Mrs. Flowers, I know the first ten amendments by heart."

"Really, say them to me." He rattled them off accurately as Mrs. Flowers read along on her paper.

"How did you memorize the amendments?"

"I just repeated them in my head while I did my worksheets. While the teacher yelled at the kids in the back making noise, I kept on repeating the amendments."

Over that three year span Ellis read every book that was in the library. He even read the books Mrs. Flowers ordered specifically for him. He taught himself Spanish and Korean. He practiced Korean with the liquor store owner's son after school when he took breaks from circling the block. He would watch the Spanish television station late at night to practice Spanish.

The summer after his eighth grade graduation he was promoted up the ranks from a Watcher to a Dealer, bringing Earl with him as his right hand man, and extra "muscle". At the age of seventeen Earl stood six-feet, four-inches tall. He weighed three hundred and thirty pounds. Earl was solid. Many people began to fear Ellis because if he told Earl to kill, he would.

When Ellis was a watcher he learned the names of all of the police officers that patrolled his block, which made dealing easy for him. He was not afraid of the cops because he knew their names. He understood that they were men just like him even though he was only fourteen. As he began to sell more drugs and get a stronger crew, he moved up the ranks of the drug hierarchy in his neighborhood. He went to school only to sell drugs, have meetings with his crew, and talk to the prettiest girls in the class. In middle school he had learned from the older drug dealers as he watched over their blocks. He also used the tactics of the great men he read about in books. By high school he began selling marijuana and crack. He used Earl to help him monopolize all drug sales.

As soon as he turned sixteen he had enough money to buy his dream car, a black Lexus. Ellis regularly got books from Mrs. Flowers. As he got deeper in the drug business he was never alone long enough to visit the library or buy books at the mall. When he went to the mall he bought clothes and shoes for himself, Earl, his brothers, and selected members of his crew.

He would give Marcus or Daniel an envelope with a book list and money for Mrs. Flowers to buy his books. He always put extra money in the envelope, but Mrs. Flowers always sent back the exact change. His brothers took the books home in their backpacks and placed them under his bed for Ellis to read as soon as he got home. His brothers loved to run errands for him, but he never allowed them to sell his drugs.

By the age of twenty, he ran all four quadrants in the District of Columbia. He was the boss of dealers in northwest, northeast, southwest, and southeast. Earl was the leader of Ellis's intimidators and killers. No one died without a head nod from Ellis. He tried to keep his head nods to a minimum because he didn't want screaming mothers to appear in his dreams as they mourned the deaths of their sons.

As a watcher he had learned the names of every new and old cop in the precinct. This knowledge gave him an edge over the other drug dealers in his neighborhood. He carefully observed the corrupt cops. He also studied the underpaid cops who wanted to buy their wives a tennis bracelet or a larger wedding ring. Ellis knew that cops made as much money as teachers, but they had perks. They could carry guns. They could beat people up in deserted alleys or in the back of police cars. The cops received gifts depending on their commitment to looking the other way and allowing him to sell his drugs without being arrested.

In each quadrant he was on very good terms with the police chief. He sent their families on cruises to Jamaica; he bought their children laptops, and paid college tuition. Depending on the favor he needed, he'd update the model of their cars, pay rent for a mistress, or pay off debts. Eventually his influence extended to the mayor and a key congressman on Capitol Hill. Ellis knew that men loved extravagance as much as women, so he showered them all with lavish gifts, especially drugs and women.

Ellis had an invisible key to the city. He loved all of his power. He knew that he could run red lights without getting pulled over. He zoomed down streets as cops waved at him as he sped by on residential streets. If a street sign read "One Way," Ellis was not afraid to drive his car down the block in the opposite direction. Nothing ever happened to him when he violated traffic laws. He always woke up for another day.

Ellis was a form of salvation for Washington D.C.'s poverty-stricken residents because he gave a great deal back to the community. He owned clothing stores on Georgia Avenue, Rhode Island, North Capitol, Florida Avenue, and on H Street. He owned two gentleman's clubs in Maryland. All of these businesses were used to launder his drug money as well as give jobs to people in the community. It was easier for him to deposit large sums of money from his clothing stores into a bank account. This stopped the bank from questioning the fluctuation of his deposits.

By this time he drove a classic seven hundred series Mercedes Benz. It had a white exterior, opaque leather interior, wood paneling, and shiny rims that kept spinning when his car was parked. His financial advisors and lawyers thought he needed a plainer American car to keep him under the radar. It didn't matter if Ellis drove an American or foreign car. His every move was watched closely and everyone knew who he was.

He bought his grandmother a house in Upper Marlborough. She loved living in a quiet neighborhood with other retired African American families. She joined a bid whist club and bought two dogs. His brothers went to high school in Upper Marlborough instead of Dunbar High School, which was Ellis's alma mater.

He moved the mother of his two sons to Columbia, Maryland into a home with six bedrooms and three baths. By selling drugs he had created the American dream for his family and his children. The house was one of four large homes on a dead-end street. He needed his three children and his wife to live a nice life away from the troubles in the ghetto's that he helped perpetuate.

He got married to the mother of his two children in his new home, in a very small ceremony with only five others present-- his grandmother, twin brothers, the preacher, and Earl. His wife's wedding ring was custom made with sapphires on each side with a large diamond in the middle. They ate his grandmother's southern-style meal after the intimate ceremony. For dessert there was an elaborate frosted and cream-filled cake from a black owned bakery in Forestville, Maryland. That night after everyone left and Tania put the children to bed, they made love as husband and wife.

Tania prompted him to use the millions of dollars he made every month from his drug business to invest in real estate. He bought single family homes in the city and apartments on the outskirts of the city. He rented the properties at decent rates to single mothers, newlyweds, and college students. None of his tenants paid more than six hundred dollars and utilities were always included.

When white families began to gentrify the neighborhoods, he had his real estate agents buy up as much property as possible. Some of the homes he sold and others he kept as the neighborhoods became more upscale. He waited to sell the homes after the property value had appreciated and ended up making five times his investment.

One night Tania smiled at him in their double king-sized bed,

"Baby, everything you do turn to gold."

"What do you mean?" Ellis wasn't confused. He loved to hear his wife stroke his ego.

"I just gave you the idea two years ago to go into the real estate business. Now you own all of those properties in Washington D.C. and at the tip of Maryland."

"You giving me the idea made me feel like I had to do a great job because you believed in me."

"I know my baby is a great businessman. Besides, I wanted our kids to own some property."

"They already do, I bought most of the properties in their names."

"Ellis, I love you," Tania smiled up at him before their tender kiss ended their conversation.

As the city began to change, it became more apparent to Ellis that he needed to stop selling drugs. His real estate business was clean and prosperous. The drug business was getting uglier and more complicated. He had to use drastic measures each day to maintain his power. The gifts were getting more expensive and the amount of blood on his hands was unbearable.

He decided that the best way to wash away all of his bad deeds was to do a very large amount of good deeds. He started to pay some tenants' rent; he knew that he couldn't give the rent money directly to each tenant. He feared that if he gave them money and said, "I want you to use this money for your rent," that they would use the money for clothes or drugs. He didn't trust the apartment owners to give everyone free month's rent, so he got money orders from a local check cashing joint and then he told one of his foot soldiers to slide the money orders under every door. He did this in every quadrant at four different apartment complexes every month.

He later found out that some of the crack heads had devised a way to cash the money orders. This disappointed him, but it was his fault that they were addicted to his drugs. He figured that money was not going to work with people who worshiped money and crack as their God. The people that he saw when he went into the ghetto would do anything for money, no matter the amount. He wasn't surprised that they had cashed the money orders because he saw women sell their bodies for less than five dollars.

One day he watched a mother try to sell her nine-year-old daughter to a pimp that she owed money. Luckily for the young girl, the pimp did not accept the offer, but the little girl still had to go home with a crazy mother. He later began to give away sandwiches to homeless people on the street. He made the boys and men in his lowest ranks deliver the sandwiches all through the city. Ellis wasn't always a nice guy especially when his people did not follow his direct orders.

One Monday everyone had to deliver sandwiches to different parts of the city. He put Pretty Boy Freddie in charge of delivering the sandwiches to the homeless people who sat outside the Martin Luther

King Library. Ellis was watching every move that Pretty Boy Freddie made. Everyone liked Freddie and he reminded Ellis of himself as a young hustler. Ellis wanted to use the boy as a face to talk to the police officers and ward leaders. This could help him slowly distance himself from the business. Pretty Boy Freddie had to show Ellis that he was trustworthy first. Delivery of the sandwiches was going to be an easy test.

Ellis drove in his white Mercedes to every sandwich drop off that he had decided on in the city. His last stop was the Martin Luther King Library before he went to his lunch meeting. He stepped out of his car in a tailored tan Armani suit and tan alligator shoes. He asked a homeless man sitting next to the book drop off box, "Did ya'll get sandwiches today?"

The man asked the woman standing behind him, "Did anyone drop off any food for us today?"

"No but, Sam found two bags full of sandwiches, by the side wall. That nigga' didn't even try to share."

Ellis gave the man and the woman twenty dollars each. He hoped that they used the money to buy something other than Mad Dog or drugs. He knew that the money he gave them would probably end up on the money roll of one of his dealers. He drove off in search of Pretty Boy Freddie. He made one phone call to Freddie's baby mama.

"Where's Pretty Boy Freddie?" His thoughts were venomous as he waited for the girl's reply.

"He right here Mr. Ellis. He high as a kite." He never understood why the younger kids called him "Mr. Ellis."

"If you keep him at your house, I'll give you money to go shopping."

"You'll give me money to go shopping, down Georgetown?"

"You have some expensive taste little girl." Ellis hung up the phone and considered the punishment that he would unleash on Freddie's ass. He wanted to hurt Freddie enough so that everyone understood that they needed to follow his orders. He called up several of his boys who loved to beat and kill.

"I need ya'll to go to Pretty Boy Freddie's girl's house and beat him senseless in the street. If anyone asks why, tell them it's because he didn't deliver Ellis' sandwiches. Tell his girl to meet me at the corner. Ay, don't hurt his face."

"Why are you protectin' his face?"

"Don't worry about my reasons, just do the job." Ellis pushed the "End" button on his phone. Pretty Boy Freddie was never going to move up the ranks. His girlfriend was too disloyal and he was going to suffer intense public humiliation. He careened his car to the corner where he had to meet Pretty Boy Freddie's baby mama. Afterward he sent the crying girl off with three hundred dollars back to watch her boyfriend get beat up. Then Ellis headed to his meeting.

Even when he tried to do good deeds, he had to turn around and do another bad deed. Every week he had some of foot soldiers hand out bags of groceries to the working women getting off the stops on the Metro Green line. He never had a problem with anyone not following any of his good deed orders, after everyone heard about Pretty Boy Freddie.

He gave turkeys out during Thanksgiving, warm clothes at the beginning of the cold months, and toys during the holiday season. He moved further away from drug selling and got more involved in his real estate business. People began to call him "Black Robin Hood" instead of "Ellis" or "Mr. Ellis". He was becoming a modern day philanthropist in the ghettos of Washington, D.C. He started to appoint different people to run his drug selling business.

His brothers, Marcus and Daniel begged to take over. He sent them to a historically black college in Atlanta, Georgia far away from the District. Earl had become his trusted lieutenant, while Ellis remained the general.

Ellis died in late August, while Washington D.C. was experiencing a series of horrible rain storms. The crickets on Elm Street were singing loudly in an eerie unison, after each clap of lightening as the rain approached. Each second the sound from the crickets got louder until the sound was hurtful. The sky was gray and hazy. Everyone retreated into the shelter of their homes as a heavy rain became more evident. Every couple of minutes thunder roared through the clouds like a woman's steady contractions during childbirth.

Flickers of lightning turned the sky from gray to white. The thunder continued to roll the clouds together. The sky turned from white to deep red, more distinct than any artist's color palette. Ellis was arguing with Earl in his white Mercedes over money.

They were parked near Ellis' old home at 2nd and Elm Street. Earl pointed a gun in Ellis's face, and then a lightning bolt cut through the sky. The soft murmur of the first gunshot was only slightly audible over the crackling lightning. The second gunshot sounded over the sheets of rain that hit the ground after the clouds burst. Earl killed Ellis by shooting him in the face, then in the heart.

Earl ran down the block, by the time he was ready to turn the corner his purple tailored suit was drenched, making it harder for him to run under the weight of the rain coupled with his shame. Ellis was slumped over his steering wheel just like he used to do when he was eleven years, watching the street with his arms over his bike handle bars.

THE SMOKER

Tessa's demeanor changed when she smoked her Newport cigarettes. She entered her own private club where the bouncers admitted only one person: Tessa Lanice Pierson. She enjoyed her solitude. She knew that she was alone, yet she was never lonely as she inhaled and exhaled. She had her own special ceremonial dance that she enjoyed with each cigarette. She tilted her head, jiggled the cigarette in between her fingers, and glided it into her mouth. She inhaled as if the cigarette were providing her last breath on earth. Her eyes never focused on anything dead or alive when she smoked. When she smoked Tessa saw everything and nothing, seeing everything and nothing gave her the most peace.

When she smoked her first cigarette of the day she always found herself reminiscing about bits of her life. Today she thought about the first time she saw Sinica before she knew his name. He was walking out of her neighborhood bodega eating a chocolate candy bar. Tessa was at the crosswalk waiting for the traffic to stop. She watched him eating his candy bar, and as he moved the candy bar to his mouth, she wished that she was the candy bar. As he took a bite of the candy bar, the caramel got stuck on his upper lip. He licked his lip from corner to yummy corner. Tessa wanted the traffic to stop immediately so that she could introduce herself and start a new love affair. He had his large hands positioned at the bottom of the wrapper. His face was in sublime bliss as his tongue caressed caramel and chocolate. He chewed slowly, savoring each bite. Tessa thought that if he took that much time with a candy bar, God only knows what he could do with her. By the time traffic had slowed enough for Tessa to cross the street, Sinica had already disappeared around the corner, and she hoped that she would get a second chance to cross paths with the luscious, young man eating the candy bar.

One day she was running late to her office building. One of those buildings that had a trillion floors and a billion companies with posh offices. The front window panes and door matched the glacier type look of the entire strip of office buildings. In the winter the mirrors reflected the light that bounced from the sun, onto the snow, then back onto the windows. On rainy days the water slid of the perfectly waxed windows with no sound. In the summertime her office building looked hot, even though the air-conditioning was on at full blast. On some summer days she had to wear a light sweater to counteract the constant chill from the air conditioning.

The lobby had wood paneling and dim lights all year long. It was always serene, despite the overweight guards who undressed the female workers with their eyes. Her job at Sweet was to insure that the magazine had the feature stories that knocked the socks off of the competition. Sweet was a new magazine. The staff at Sweet, including Tessa, focused on articles about subjects that really pushed sales, and enhanced the magazine's image and popularity. Today she was writing an article about, "Finding a Man Who Loves a Strong and

Successful Women." Every month Tessa attempted to prove that Sweet magazine was the new voice of young women attempting to lead fabulous lives.

All Sweet's employees prided themselves on arriving early and leaving late. This morning Tessa was extremely late. It was almost lunch time as she passed the windows and entered the mahogany-paneled lobby.

She reached the front door of the building at the same time it swung open. Eager to find the source of her convenience, she looked to her right to see a fine parka, crisp jeans, and Timberland-wearing brother graciously opening the door, "Slow down! You can't turn back time."

She remembered him immediately as the guy eating the candy bar. She strutted through the door as if it was seven a.m. and no one was preparing for lunch. She had to take herself out of work mode and into strut-your-stuff-and-work-that-thang mode quickly or she would have to hope for a third opportunity to get a chocolaty lick of candy bar man.

Tessa thought he had disappeared. She looked over her shoulder to see him walking to her stride and checking out her curves. He was only behind her to check out her ass ...ets. Out the corner of her eye she could see the security guards joining in on the show.

When she reached the elevator he pushed the "Up" button for her. She gave him her, "Thank you" smile. He gave his, "It's no problem. I'm happy to oblige" wave, as he smoothly moved the backside of his hand up and over. Tessa thought she was in a 1940's Rita Hayworth movie.

Tessa wished the elevator was slow on this morning, but the doors opened immediately. She wanted to stand next to him a little longer. He had passed all of the tests. He opened the front door, pressed the elevator button, smiled, and smelled good. She thought that at least she should be able to spend a little more time with him.

Tessa stepped into the elevator alone and immediately craved a cigarette, especially since she had blown her second chance to get to know candy bar man. As the elevator doors closed, Tessa scolded herself for not getting her new friend's name. Unfortunately she would have to wait until she took a break from writing her latest article to start an investigation on her new friend.

After about an hour of daydreaming about candy bar guy, she came to the conclusion that she had a flaming new crush. Now she had to think of schemes to see him again.

Then she saw her candy man's Timberland boots first-- then the mail cart.

Her new crush was the new mail delivery guy.

Her building changed mail guys every few weeks.

Damn. Damn. Damn. Her fantasies about his occupation were shattered. He wasn't a writer, a reporter, or a photographer.

He must have sensed her surprise and apprehension,

"So you made it to your office."

"Yes." If anyone overheard Tessa's conversation they would have thought she had heard some very bad news.

"I'm Sinica," he said with a charming smile as he handed her a stack of mail.

"Do I have anything else?" her tone was utterly indifferent, almost crass.

Sinica began to write something on an envelope. Tessa sat quietly as she remembered that she hadn't ordered a signature upon delivery item.

"I don't remember ordering anything that I had to sign for."

"This is what came for you, Ms...."

"Tessa Pierson"

He handed her the envelope and pen as if he desperately depended on her signature.

Tessa looked at the envelope.

The top line: *You are gorgeous.*

The bottom line. *May I have your number please?*

She finally smiled and even laughed at his method to get her digits. She signed the envelope quickly with her name and number, quickly before she could change her mind.

Sinica called her that night. They discovered that they lived on the same block. That evening they decided to go to the neighborhood coffee shop to talk in person over blended mochas and pound cake. Tessa and Sinica ended up talking until the owner finished cleaning up the entire restaurant including their table. In the beginning they enjoyed each other as good friends talking every day for hours after work or when he dropped off the mail.

Sinica knew that Tessa had a problem with his mail boy status. Tessa thought Sinica couldn't handle her rising publishing executive status. About eight months into their affair he began to send her mushy e-cards over the Internet. Tessa loved every e-card he sent her; she made a special folder on her e-mail file to save all of Sinica's cards.

Sinica snapped her out of her reminiscing, as he rolled over to hug his pillow tighter. Sinica was the best lover Tessa had ever had, but she didn't love him. She knew that he wanted her to love him. He had put in so much work and had done all the right things. Sinica had taken her to museums and plays that she knew he couldn't afford on his salary. They got into their worst argument the first and last time she tried to pay for their dinner. He paid in silence and he got up from the table without waiting for her. She was putting on her jacket as she looked through the restaurant window and saw Sinica staring into the street.

All she could think about was, that if their fight was bad enough she could break their relationship off. Tessa didn't want to unleash her attitude, but Sinica was definitely riding her 'tude button. Hard.

"What is the problem, Sinica?" her left hand was going for her waist, but it landed on her purse strap. She settled for the less confrontational pose.

"Tessa, I am courting you. Let me court you," he glared.

"Sweetie, you can always court me. You don't have to get so angry."

"I'm not angry," he said as he reached for her hand so that they could cross the street. "I just would like to wear the pants and I want you to carry a purse. Stop worrying about how I pay for everything, baby girl, just enjoy us being together."

"Well if I carry the purse, does that mean I can't at least go for my purse?"

"Of course, but when I say 'I got it', with my credit card in my hand, then chill out."

"How do you pay for everything?" Tessa's pace began to slow down.

They eventually stopped walking. They had stopped in front of a construction site. Tessa leaned her back against the fence. Her shoes made a 'shish' noise as she positioned herself on the fence. Sinica grabbed the part of the fence closer to her right ear. She smelled his cologne for the second time that night and she felt her blood rush through her body. She tilted her head back to help the blood rush toward her head. Even though they were fussing, she couldn't help smiling at Sinica. His charm was working on her; she wanted to show him how much it was working as soon as she locked the door of her apartment. Tessa had to end their mini-fight, quickly.

"Just answer my question honestly."

Sinica gazed into her eyes with tenderness and sincerity. "I have three jobs, which help me save my money. During the day I deliver the mail. Three nights a week I work at a retail store, and on weekend's I fix other peoples computers."

Tessa had to thank her selective memory for forgetting about all the things he did during the week.

She was so concerned with him getting a status-y type job, that she conveniently forgot that Sinica was a blue-collar hustler.

"Tessa", he looked down into her eyes, catching them before they went over his right ear.

"I really like you. You are so perfect for me. I feel like I have met my match."

"Would you like to match me…at my apartment?"

"Will our match happen on your mattress?'

"Only, if it doesn't start in the hallway first."

Sinica grabbed Tessa's hand as they began to walk down the street. Other people smiled as the two lovers passed. The closer they got to her apartment the more they groped each other.

Again, Sinica shifted in the bed, stopping another good memory, and she took another drag of her cigarette. She hated to see him in the morning light, he looked like a boy. In the morning light he didn't look like the man who sent her into total ecstasy. She touched the bottom of the ocean and the edge of the sky when Sinica was inside her. At night, his face was so determined, so focused, so manly, so caring, and so real. If only he was the same during the day as he was at night. She would probably chain Sinica to her bed and never let him leave.

She took another drag of her cigarette as more daylight crept in through the windows. She nudged Sinica awake. He woke up with a boyish smile, "Good morning Pumpkin." She smiled and pointed to his clothes hanging on one of her chairs. He dressed as she watched him cover his smooth brown body. His boxers covered his ample package of manhood and stopped at his navel. His pants covered his strong legs and his shirt masked his powerful arms. Sinica was definitely a son of the gods. He felt her eyes rove over his body,

"I really don't have to leave and I am available to stay so that you can touch."

She took another drag of her cigarette and exhaled while shaking her head, "No". She led him to the door. He begged to stay. His request fell on deaf ears. The mini- fight they had the previous night had ruined their relationship. Tessa realized then that they hadn't really dealt with any of their relationship issues.   After their fight Tessa decided she only wanted to have sex with Sinica. The good memories were annoying.

She unlocked her door with an assertive twist, opened it, and ushered Sinica out. She closed the door as soon as he passed through the threshold, his back was facing her. Her cigarette was finally out.

She walked to her kitchen and made an omelet, toast, and poured orange juice. As she was eating her phone rang. Her mother was calling to, "Just talk". She lit another cigarette because she dreaded the, "Just talk" calls. They were so one sided. Her mother just rambled on about her life. The conversation always went in the same order: her mother's love life, her garden, the office, and her siblings. Her mother's love life was so tragic. Any and every man was treated as a potential true love and great romance.

Listening to her talk about her love life was like listening to a sixteen-year-old. Her mother didn't grasp that dating is less about love and more about power struggles. After the struggles are over then love becomes important again. Some men still act like boys, some say anything, some are mean, and some are conniving. The men that her mom dated weren't always attractive, according to her sister. Her mom accepted any man's advances as long as she received some sort of affection. She hated that her mom was so needy. She just smoked her cigarettes while her mom gabbed away.

Her mom didn't even know that she smoked. Her mom didn't answer her questions or address any of Tessa's comments. If her mom were open to her daughter's advice, Tessa would tell her to remember her intuition, be selective, act like a lady, and always remember that she was nobility. She hated that her mother treated her like a friend instead of a daughter. Her silence was probably the reason that her mom and grandmother called her "aloof". She laughed at the label because her mom and grandmother really did not know her.

She was so talkative, her advice was always accurate, and her friends adored her. She made the most awful situations hilarious. She smiled and smoked. She knew that her mother only labeled her as aloof to reject the reality that her daughter was an adult, a person, and truly unique.

Her mother did the same thing every conversation, toward the end she always asked, "How are you doing?" as if it pained her.

"I'm fine. I'm going to have a gathering tonight, so I have to go to the--"

Her mom interrupted her, Tessa inhaled.

Her mom finally ended gabbing. "I'll talk to you later, I'm about to get some bird feed for the bird houses. Talk to you later, Sweetie."

"Bye, Mom." She exhaled.

The "Just Talk" was over. Her mom wasn't interested in her life as usual. She just smiled and took the last pull of her cigarette. She went to her bathroom to take a shower. In the shower she made her mental "To do" list: go to the cleaners, the wine shop, and the flower shop. When she got out the shower she had missed Sinica's voice mail message:

"Hey, Baby. You know I really don't

understand you. The crazy part is that.........

I love you and you hate me. I have been

holding in my feelings for too many months,

now. We had a great night and you kicked

me out. I really needed to stay with you

today. You are my true sunshine. I can only

have you sometimes. That hurts me deep,

baby girl. Call me back in the next hour. I

need you. I really need you..."

She looked at her watch. It was 10 a.m. She decided she would call Sinica later that afternoon, after she finished her errands. He was so melodramatic at times that it was scary and funny. She walked to her dresser decided on her outfit. She grabbed her favorite jeans and her crispest white t-shirt. She put on her make–up. Her hardest dilemma was whether to wear the diamonds or the pearls. Her job at "Sweet" was beginning to pay off. She opted for the diamonds and her newest Tiffany set. She admired herself in the mirror. She stared at her shape, her glistening skin, and her full plump lips. She smiled, grabbed her purse, and her dry cleaning.

On her way out of her apartment building she walked past Mr. Henry. "Good Morning Mr. Henry. How are you today?"

"It's a beautiful day. I'm just enjoying my retirement. And yourself?"

"The day is just beginning, but so far I'm in love with today."

His little chair began to creak as he leaned back, "I hope today stays good because I don't want to see anything bad."

"Same here. Have a very good day Mr. Henry."

Tessa thought Mr. Henry was so cute. He had been retired for seventeen years and every time she saw him he told her that he was enjoying his retirement. Tessa lit a cigarette and decided to get rid of her extra baggage, so she headed towards the dry cleaners. The street hustlers were already standing at their posts. She had to pass them to get to the cleaners. One guy stood on the right of the group and another stood on the left. Two stood across the street to see further down the street, on all sides.

As she glided down block, the street hustlers gawked, open mouthed at her beauty.

Every time she had to walk by them one tried to get her attention. Each time she passed them she saw a new face, probably fresh from the penitentiary. She knew that this crew was tight knit. All the new faces were really old faces that kept the crew intact. She had a few steps before she had to decide on her mean or happy face. With a happy face she would probably hear something slick like:

"Can I go home with you? Just so I can see your smile more often."

The mean face would only make one of the hustlers say:

"Smile. It can't be that bad." All of them would nod in unison, waiting for a glimmer of a smile.

She gave the smile because it was a beautiful day and she had a great night.

On her way to the liquor store she saw Joseph riding his bike. He was the neighborhood errand boy. *I'd rather him run errands for the adults than, him getting involved with the streets hustlers.* Tessa thought.

At any point in the day someone would yell Joseph's name down the street or the little kids playing outside were sent on a mission to find Joseph. Joseph did everything from walk the dogs to carry groceries. She was so happy to see Joseph on his bike across the street.

"What are you doing right now?"

"Nothing, Ms. Tessa. Whachoo need?"

"Could you wait for me outside the cleaners? I need you to carry my bags from the wine shop."

"Sure," Joseph leaned to the side with his kick stand and began to stare at everyone on the street.

Joseph was excited about making some more money. He knew Tessa was going to give him at least three dollars for helping her with her bags. He began to calculate his earnings from helping the old ladies and walking the white folks' dogs. He looked up to see two men fighting on a roof top. When his eyes finally adjusted he recognized one of the two arguing men. He was the rapper who called himself the "Young Disciple". Joseph thought his rapping skills were the best on the planet. As Joseph began to remember the heated rap contests Young Disciple won in the park, the other man pushed the rising rap star over the ledge, and his arms began flailing in the thin air.

Joseph started peddling toward the Young Disciple as if he could catch him on his handle bars. He knew that the man was going to die as soon as the ground jumped up to catch him. Young Disciple hit the earth with a horrific thud, like a 200 pound sack of potatoes dropping from the sky. A crowd began to surround the dead young man.

Mr. Henry had taken his hat off when he noticed the two men fighting. He knew that the argument was a very dangerous one. The way the two men were hollering and gesturing toward each other, only a trained negotiator would be able to intervene. Mr. Henry stood up when he saw the shorter young man push the taller young man over the edge. As he walked toward the falling young man he felt himself extending his arms. He let his arms drop back to his sides as soon as he realized that he had to watch the young man rapidly approach his fate--death. Mr. Henry knew that his arms were not strong enough to catch the young man.

Tessa stepped out of the cleaners looking for Joseph. She saw him peddling towards the crowd in the middle of the street. She walked cautiously toward the crowd. A woman walked past her saying, "Suicide, is the worst to deal with."

On her right Joseph and Mr. Henry stood next to each other. On her left she heard sirens far away take off toward a different emergency. Tessa knew that an ambulance was not going to come for another fifteen minutes. She saw Mr. Henry and Joseph pointing to the rooftop nodding their heads. While, a woman kept repeating "Life couldn't have been that hard". She couldn't get through the crowd. Instead she walked over to Mr. Henry and Joseph.

"What happened?" Tessa's voice was low and controlled. She felt that this was not an ordinary suicide.

Mr. Henry felt relief that she had missed his silly gesture in extending his hands in a futile attempt to catch the young man.

"She didn't see it, she was in the store," Joseph commented.

"What was 'it'?" Tessa wanted answers quickly so she could stop feeling a knot growing tighter and tighter in her stomach.

Mr. Henry added with low tone much unlike him, "That young man was pushed from the rooftop."

"What do you mean pushed?"

"He was arguing with another young man and he was pushed over the edge."

"Mr. Henry, you have to tell the police what you saw."

"Ms. Tessa, that would not be good for Mr. Henry," Joseph's wisdom was budding beyond his years.

"Anything could happen, if we told what we saw. We may have a few white neighbors, but we still have to follow the street code."

"Joseph, there is no code of honor for murder."

"I'm just a kid. I want to live to be Mr. Henry's age."

"Joseph, boy, how long have you lived on this earth?" Mr. Henry had recovered his regular vocal tone.

"We're going to tell the police that, that young man jumped, but only if they ask."

"Yup."

Tessa began to walk through the crowd, which had gotten smaller. People got tired of waiting for the police and the dead man's blood was starting to curdle under the hot summer sun. Right before she reached the man's head, she realized that the dead man was Sinica.

Everyone heard the sirens slowly approaching. By the time the detective arrived with the police no one was around to give the police a report. Tessa felt helpless. There was nothing she could do to roll back time and get some redemption for Sinica. To the police he was just another dead, young, black thug in the city. The medical examiner handed Sinica's wallet to the detective. The detective placed the wallet in a Ziploc bag. The detective smoked a quick cigarette before heading back to the precinct.

Joseph kept shaking his head as he stood next to Tessa on her front stoop, holding her bag of wines.

"Joseph, why are you shaking your head?"

"The man that died was the Young Disciple. He just signed a record deal. You haven't heard his song on the radio: "I'm in love with a girl that makes me want to light candles, and ramble, about adult things, life and her new diamond ring.'"

"No I haven't heard it, I usually only listen to my CD's."

"Ms. Tessa you should listen to the radio more. The Young Disciple has the hottest song on the radio."

"How long has he been on the radio?"

"For about two months. I bet when his album comes out it will go platinum. Do you think he was telling the truth about the girl he loved?"

"I wouldn't doubt it." Tessa had to keep herself from breaking down into pieces on her front doorstep as Joseph waved his hand then peddled down the street.

Tessa thought about Sinica as she walked to her apartment. He was in love with her. He had a record deal and a song on the radio about the love he wanted to share with her. If she had just called back, Sinica would be walking with her into her apartment.

She opened her new pack of cigarettes, lit one, and then the phone rang. Her mother's number came up on the caller ID. She answered the phone and the second "Just talk" of the day began. The conversation followed the same order: her mother's love life; her garden; the office and her siblings. Tessa smoked to stop the heavy silent tears and the crushing pains radiating from her heart. She held the receiver to her ear while she listened to her mother talk as if she was the only woman in the world with a story to tell.

OUR ATTIC

To this day I believe that my mother and I are very blessed. When my grandmother, Nana, died from breast cancer she left my mom and I, her house on 25th and Adams in Los Angeles, California. Her house was immense, with windows in every room, five bedrooms, and three bathrooms. There was a breakfast nook with bay windows surrounding the large breakfast table. On their twentieth wedding anniversary my grandfather built a small, half circular bench along the wall of the bay windows, for my grandmother. He even built wooden flowerpot holders so that my grandmother could plant flowers in the house.

My grandmother's will, left the house to my mother, her youngest child. My Uncle Louis inherited my grandfathers' boat. My Uncle Gregory got the recreation vehicle and my Aunt Janice gladly accepted the gold Cadillac. She loved to ride in it on Sunday afternoons. After everything was finalized Louis, Gregory, and Janice sold their inheritance from my grandmother to the highest bidder. When they noticed that my mother wasn't going to sell the house they tried to pressure her into putting the house on the market.

"We can move you and Adam to a new house in Fontana." Janice smiled hard at my mother. We could all hear the urgency of her tone. My aunt saw the big house as an investment.

"Why do you think I'd want to move to Fontana? Anyway, I'm not selling Mama's house. Mama and

Daddy would cry for the rest of eternity if I sold this house. I still don't understand why ya'll sold everything already."

Nana could have left the house to anyone in the family, but her first choice was my mother Patricia. At our last family barbecue before my grandmother died, she boasted to my uncles and aunt,

"This is my most loyal child. She is always trying to make my life easier and she cooks for me on Sundays. If it wasn't for her, I'd be watching television instead of eating at this barbecue."

My mother's two older brothers and her eldest sister stared at her with jealous grins, while she was praised. My grandmother was telling the truth. My Uncle Louis was an alcoholic. He was in and out of rehab. Louis always smelled of liquor and moldy bread. Everyone knew that he never recovered from losing his wife Sydney. Sydney brought me gifts for all of my birthdays until she died after I turned nine. Louis loved Sydney because she was, beautiful, smart, funny, and fearless. She owned her own event planning business. She was always planning a beautiful wedding or anniversary party. Sydney used to make my uncle's eyes shine when she talked to him at our family gatherings.

I remembered the day my Uncle Louis called my mother to tell her the bad news. I was staring out my window with glee because it rarely hailed in Los Angeles. On my way to our front lawn after the hail stopped, I walked past my mother sitting on our yellow floral couch crying. I stopped with my hand on the doorknob,

"Mommy, what's the matter?"

"Louis and Sydney were in a car accident. Louis is okay but, Sydney is dead."

I walked to my mother and put my small arm around her neck. I held my head down to cry.

A couple of days later we were at the funeral. Uncle Louis entered the funeral stumbling over his feet with a clear bottle in his hand.

He was yelling, "I shouldn't have tried that shortcut on San Vicente." My Uncle Louis hasn't stopped drinking since the funeral and he never went back to finish his residency at the hospital.

My other Uncle Gregory is always pestering my mother with get-rich quick scams. After he graduated from college, he went into the restaurant business with three of his friends. The restaurant was a great success, but one of his partners took money out of their joint business account, and then left the state with two years of earnings. After this debacle, my uncle had to start from the beginning to make the same type of money he made from the restaurant.

One night I overheard my mother talking with my Aunt Janice on our apartment's patio, "Gregory called me in the middle of the night tryin' to sell me herbal juice."

"Patricia, I know. He tried to get me to become an associate for some long distance phone carrier."

"Do you think those schemes work?"

"Of course they work for people that stay dedicated twenty four hours a day for three or more years. Gregory doesn't stay long enough to reap the rewards."

"I wish he would stop calling us to jump start his business."

"He is just trying to help us out while we help him."

My aunt understood her brother because she was a real estate agent. She was always on the hunt for prime real estate. My grandmother's house was prime real estate. At our monthly Sunday dinners at my grandmother's house before she died, my aunt always tried to coax my grandmother into selling her house.

"Mama, you could get so much money for selling this house. We can sell the house and move you to one of those new houses in Fontana."

"Girl, What I want with some Fontana?"

"Your father built the table that you eating on right now. You've been eaten' on that table since you was a baby. All a' ya'll, even the new little ones. Most of the furniture in this house was built with your father's bare hands. Why would I sell a house that holds all this love and history?"

My aunt stuffed her mouth with some sweet potatoes thinking of a retort that never made it past her fork. All the adults knew that she was going to ask again at the next dinner. My grandmother knew that if she left the house to anyone else besides my mother, my aunt would have sold the family's home rickety split.

I stayed at my grandmother's house every weekend before she died. I loved waking up with my cousins and running down to the breakfast nook to eat breakfast. The kitchen had an island in the middle. My grandmother told us during our weekend stays,

"We were the first family on the block with a kitchen counter in the middle of the kitchen."

When we walked into the house, we were always greeted by a long foyer decorated with family pictures, and anonymous embroidered quotes. My favorite quote was "Home, Sweet, and Home." I remembered reading that quote with a feeling of great accomplishment after I first learned how to read. No one ever crossed the threshold of the living room. All the seats were upholstered with a flowery, red fabric, and covered in plastic. There were black and white pictures of women wearing carefully combed chignons and men with straight parts down the center of their scalps. The pictures in the room added to its off-limits appeal. This led my cousins and me to devise ways to play in the room without being detected.

One day we all gathered the courage to follow my oldest cousin Rufus into the living room. He only walked two steps into the room before my little cousin Tanya hollered,

"Oooohh, you made foot prints!" We all ran towards the stairs as we heard our grandmother from the side patio off of the dining room,

"Why ya'll children makin' all a' that noise?" We all froze as we heard her chair creak back into place before she began walking toward the stairs. She approached us with her loving smile and probing eyes. After she had forced all of us to stare at the floor, she walked closer to the living room. She stopped at the door, "Who be'n in my livin' room?"

We never answered her even after she had waited in silence for our replies. No one snitched on Rufus, but we all had to suffer his punishment. We were all separated into different sections of the house. We all missed two prime hours of playing outside.

Nana put me in the seat at the top of the stairs landing on the second floor, directly underneath her attic. We never tried to walk into the attic. I had only seen the ladder leading to the attic a few times. It was usually open when one of my uncles dusted. I'd hear light thuds or the brush of brooms as they cleaned the attic floors. The only other time I saw the attic open was when my mother took shoeboxes up the stairs, the first Sunday dinner after my birthday. I always wondered what those shoe boxes contained. She always looked so relieved when she descended the stairs. I never questioned her about the boxes because I was usually playing with my cousins and I figured it was related to one of those mysterious adult secrets.

After my grandmother died my mother and I moved into the house that held so many memories from my childhood. My mother used to cry every night after we moved in, but she stopped crying in front of me after about a year. I don't think she ever really stopped crying, I think she held her tears until her bedroom door was closed. Instead of crying constantly, she poured all her energy into the maintenance of the house. She cleaned rigorously every weekend.

With each changing season she cleaned underneath furniture, in dusty crevices, and even the roof shingles. She really worked hard to maintain the immaculate appearance of the living room. She hired a wood floor service to wax the hardwood floors every year. She reupholstered old furniture to accentuate the Victorian era identity of the house, but still added some of her contemporary decorating ideas. She kept fresh plants in the flower pots in the breakfast nook. She cooked a big Sunday dinner once a month and we maintained our family annual barbecue.

My mother started a breast cancer support group in memory of my grandmother. She traveled to different conventions and gatherings around the city advocating breast cancer awareness for African American women. In October, she invited business contacts and influential people to our house for a silent auction. I would have to stay at my Uncle Gregory's house with my cousins. A babysitter would tend to all the kids who were too young to help at the fundraiser.

By the time I was twelve, she gave me more household chores to help her with the up keep of the house. I didn't mind any of my chores, because I knew that my grandmother was so proud that my mother was taking care of her house. My friends used to tease me because I couldn't play outside until I had finished all of my chores. I never paid attention to their teasing until I had to clean the attic. Every six months my mother made me clean out the attic. The first time I cleaned out the attic I found a dead mouse on a sticky trap.

Our attic is a labyrinth of towering stacks of boxes lined with dust. It smelled like old books and papers. The dust gets very thick in the attic because it is only cleaned twice a year. My mother kept the windows closed to keep out nesting birds and insects. The mice always found a way to make a home in the attic, but they never ventured to other parts of the house. Whenever I cleaned I never saw any live mice. I figured they probably hid behind the heavier boxes. I just crossed my fingers as I cleaned because I didn't want to see any mice running along the base boards of our attic.

All the boxes were filled with family mementos and keep sakes. Some boxes had yearbooks, trophies, and school pictures. There were boxes of trophies that couldn't fit into trophy cases. Every time I earned a trophy from baseball or football my mother would remove the oldest trophy and make me put it in my 'Trophy box' in the attic. My cousins would bring their old trophies with them to Sunday dinners following the end of all the different sports seasons.

Every six months I grabbed the broom, mop, duster, and bucket to finish the last of my chores. I ascended the stairs into the attic and prepared my nostrils for dust mites. I opened the window to start the air circulating, and then I started sweeping from corner to corner. After sweeping the visible portions of the floor, I had to move all the boxes to get the dust underneath each tower of boxes. Over six months without any visitors besides one of us kids dumping a trophy, makes our attic collect a lot of dust.

I started at the tower of boxes deep in the corner of the attic; the boxes were extremely dusty because I never really cleaned them as extensively as the boxes closer to the attic door. My mother never walked to that section of the attic when she looked over my finished cleaning job. I made sure to keep the trophy boxes as dust free as possible, as well as the boxes containing everyone's high school mementos.

In order to deep clean the tower of boxes, I had to lift each box one at a time. I moved the first box with ease because it was the lightest. I took my shirt off because I used any opportunity to show off my chest, even if I was in the attic alone. My years of playing football had molded my body into great athletic shape. I bench pressed the most weight during football camp and my coaches knew that I could probably snag a division one football scholarship.

I was in a rush to play football in the park, I was cleaning carelessly. I wanted to meet my friends at the park for a tackle football game, we didn't use any pads. Every weekend at the park we figured out who had the strongest tackle by the force we used to bring our opponent down to the ground. I held the crown for tackling the hardest.   The week before I forced the running back to lose the ball, I smacked him so hard that the ball popped out of his hand like he had butter slathered on his fingers. I didn't want to do any extra work because I needed to get to the park to maintain my status as the hardest tackler in the neighborhood.

When I moved to the second tower of boxes it toppled over exposing carefully stacked envelopes, enclosed in shoeboxes. As I picked up the envelopes I noticed they were all unopened. I turned one over and noticed that the letter was addressed to me, Adam Campbell Jr. I always thought that it was funny that I was a "junior" to someone that I had never met. No one called me "Junior", but it was the official name in my school records and on my birth certificate.

My mother never called me "Junior". She told me one morning while we were eating breakfast in the breakfast nook,

"Honey, when you turn eighteen you can change your name."

"I like my name mom. I'm just going to take off that junior part."

"That's the name you were given."

As usual my mother quickly exited the room to end the conversation because I wasn't going to end the conversation until I got acceptable answers. She picked up her plate with half an English muffin left. She was in such a rush that she left her coffee on the table. I finished my steak and potatoes alone and concentrated on my upcoming football game. I had to stop thinking about a man I had never met; I needed all my energy to hit the other team. I decided to use the disdain I had for my father on the other team. That night I made twelve sacks, a new record for sacks made by a high school lineman in the Los Angeles city section division.

I felt that same anger as I stood in the attic, reading the name in the return section of the envelope, Adam

Campbell, Sr.   I had never been given one of these letters that were stored away in shoe boxes, in the furthest corner of our attic.   I never knew anything about my father because my mother avoided conversations about him.   When I got the courage to ask, "Who was my father?" She either yelled at me, or quickly left the room which usually ended the conversation.   I learned when I was younger to let adults keep some of their adult secrets.   This was one of the secrets that I had to chisel at very slowly every couple of months.

One day she actually replied to my question with simmering anger, "Why do you want to know about him?"   I wanted to say, "Because he is my father, and I want to know if we look alike. I'm curious." But today was different. I didn't need the courage to ask my mother the mystery about my father. The mystery about my father was trapped in these hundreds of closed envelopes. All I had to do was open one and read. The box was packed with filled shoe boxes of letters addressed to me, Adam Campbell, Jr.

My father had missed my first day of school, my first fight, my first kiss, my first sack, and my first touchdown. He had missed my entire life. He never saw my perfect report cards or phenomenal performances on the football field.

While my thoughts took me deeper into my childhood, I had started to organize the letters. I unconsciously put the letters in order according to the post office delivery date.   I felt my eyes water when I realized my father had written a letter for me every week since I was in the first grade.

I didn't know which envelope to open first. I didn't know if I should start with the most recent letters or with the first letter my father ever sent? As I put the letters in order, some of the envelopes were marked, "Do not bend, photos." It was easier for me to open the envelopes that contained pictures than the letters. I didn't know what to expect. After I pulled out the pictures, I let them fall to the floor as I leaned onto another tower of boxes for support. The man who stared from the pictures into my eyes looked exactly like me. We had the same shaped head, eyes, and nose. Our lips were shaped differently; I had my mother's heart-shaped, full lips.

I took the first box of letters along with the picture that revealed the identity of my father with me as I carefully walked down the stairs. This new revelation of my father's existence was making me light-headed. I really wanted to go to my room and sleep. I knew that it was time to get some answers from my mother. I found my mother in the breakfast nook, watering the plants in my grandmother's flower pot. I plopped down into a chair and waited for her to finish watering the second plant,

"Are you hungry?"

"No. Mom".

She turned around quickly to decipher my horrible tone. When she turned around she saw me removing the dust from the top of the shoebox.

"What are you doing?"

"I was cleaning the attic until I found a box full of letters."

"From, who?"

"You know who. From Adam, my father."

"You weren't supposed to find that box." "Well I found it Mom." I was using more base in my voice than I usually did when speaking with my mother.

"Don't use that tone with me, little boy."

"Mom, tell me what's going on."

"It's a difficult story to tell."

"Start from the beginning."

"God wants you to know, I have to tell you now. Honey, I loved your father with all my heart and soul. He was what you would call a rolling stone or a player." He had a lot of girlfriends, but I was the only one that got pregnant. I loved him hard before my pregnancy. When he would take me out we enjoyed each other's company, but he didn't want to settle down. When I got pregnant he accused me of trying to trap him into marriage. I was hurt by his accusation. He tried to get me to get an abortion, of course, I refused. He stopped taking me out when he realized that I was going to keep you. By my seventh month of pregnancy he stopped calling or visiting me. I didn't start hearing from him until you started the first grade. He called a couple of weeks before you started school, we had a horrible argument. I told him to stop calling, but he said that he was going to mail you letters to grandma's house."

"Why didn't grandma give me the letters?"

"I didn't let her. Every day I stopped by to check the mail after work. Whenever I found the letter from your father in the mail, I'd hide them in an empty shoebox."

I remembered watching my mother take shoeboxes up the ladder to the attic.

"Your father is very stubborn and he kept sending you letters."

"Letters that I never got Mom," my voice began to crack.

"Do you want to read the letters?"

"Yes"

"Or, do you want to call your father?"

"You know his number?"

Her voice was coated in shame, "Yes."

As angry and hurt as I was with my mother I asked her, "Will you read the letters with me first before we call?"

"Of course."

The first letter began, *"Son I'm sure you know how to read. I need to tell you that I love you."* My father had filled the letters with stories of his new family, my brothers, sisters, and new house. I noticed my mother tense up when I read stories of my father's other family. He ended each letter, *"If you ever want to come visit my door is always open for you, Bubba."* By the time we stopped reading through each letter it was three in the morning and we had only read the letters that corresponded with my first year in junior high. My eyes were red from crying as I read each letter.

My father continued to reach out to me through his letters even though my mother tried to keep us apart. The letters revealed that my father lived in Inglewood, California on Fifth Avenue, on one of the streets that had contest to see who could have the best Christmas decorations. Every Christmas my Uncle Louis sobered up enough to take my cousins and me on a holiday excursion to Inglewood. We had passed my father's house every year since my Uncle Louis had started the tradition.

My mom offered to drive me to his house as I prepared for bed.

I told her, "Mom, I want to read all the letters first before I go to meet him. I don't think I'm ready, but you can invite him to my next football game. I'll take care of everything after that."

My mother invited my father to my football game. He sat in the stands, extremely proud. After the game he gave me a long hug. I could see his tears under his sunglasses. From that day on we were inseparable. He drove me to college for my freshman year. We talk three times a week and we spend holidays together at my Grandmother's house.

AUTHOR BIO

Taaji Rauf is a writer and educator. She is writing her first how-to book, a novel, and her next collection of short stories. This has been an amazing journey for her. She wishes, hopes, and prays that you have enjoyed Before Life. In the near future you will be able to enjoy many, many more of her books. Taaji lives in Los Angeles, California, writing, teaching, and enjoying life.

Booking, Inquiries, and Contact:

www.taajirauf.weebly.com
taajirauf@gmail.com
www.twitter.com/crownkindqueen
www.facebook.com/taajirauf